HER DEVOTED **HERO**
A BLACK DAWN NOVEL

BY CAITLYN O'LEARY

DEDICATION

To those who do serve and have served.
Thank You.

SYNOPSIS

Navy SEAL Dex Evans has a problem. His buddies think it's a riot when they sign him up for a dating service behind his back. But who would have thought that with a profile like SailorBoy69 he'd snag a woman who was hysterically funny and gorgeous? Too bad she was also skittish as all hell. Dex fears that when she finds out his profile was a set-up, his happily ever after could sink to the bottom of the ocean.

Single mother, Kenna Wright was in way over her head. She'd spent years putting her child first while ignoring her needs. So, what was she thinking responding to the flirtatious email? Luckily for her, when she is stuck on a project with Dex, he's even better in person than he'd been on his online profile. But can she believe this sexy SEAL when he says he's looking for more than a fling?

When one of her co-workers is murdered, and it looks like Kenna might be the next one in the killer's crosshairs, Dex is determined to keep her safe. But with a target on her back, it's really hard to keep a shield over her heart.

CHAPTER ONE

The motto of the Navy SEAL's was 'The Only Easy Day is Yesterday.' Dex Evans had watched the members of Midnight Delta, a rival SEAL team, drop like flies as they fell in love. So, he and his buddies from Black Dawn had cooked up the idea of making a new motto for them. They'd crossed out the normal team logo and inserted 'Happily Ever After is Possible' on a banner and hung it between two of their trucks so that it was waiting for them the day the naval carrier docked in San Diego. An entire ship of sailors and SEALs had seen the damn thing that morning in the harbor. Two months later, and the men were still giving the Midnight Delta team a ration of shit.

That prank had been a highlight that warmed Dex's heart.

It least it had been until he had opened his personal e-mail in-box.

Dex sat back with his second beer and did what he'd been doing for the last four nights, politely telling persistent women, that his identity had been hacked and he hadn't really reached out to them on the CaliSingles dating site. Most of the women took it well, but out of the two hundred and twenty-eight women that he'd contacted so far, seventeen had been angry and bitter, and two had been downright scary.

He was almost done with this project, and ready to start plotting his revenge on the technical guru of Midnight Delta. But he couldn't quite seem to force himself to hit send on the last rejection e-mail. He looked at the woman's picture again.

She was cute.

She had a hint of an overbite that was a real turn-on when you paired it with her long strawberry blonde hair. But come on, he'd seen at least twenty women with more beautiful photos. Still, there was something about this girl who called herself 'SNMP.'

He'd laughed his ass off when he'd read what she'd written. None of the others made him almost spit up his beer.

He re-read her introductory letter.

Hello SailorBoy69,

SNMP stands for So Not Mary Poppins. Take it to heart. My photo is me, but it's pretty much a fake since it took me two hours and twenty dollars worth of product to achieve the look. If we were to meet in person, I probably wouldn't look anywhere close to this, soak in this picture. Actually, don't worry, we won't meet, but I'll get to that.

Here's me in a nutshell. I live in the good part of town because I work my ass off handling my full-time job as a nurse, plus a part-time gig. I do this so my son can go to school in a decent school district. Being a good mother is the single most important thing in my life, I have no earthly idea why I'm responding to your profile since I don't have time to date. Did I mention I have a kid, two jobs and really don't look like this?

I like the fact that you're serving our country. That's part of the reason I'm reaching out to you. But the real reason I'm writing is that I'm ninety-nine-point nine percent sure you won't respond, so this is a safe letter to write. I can feel good that I've finally put myself out there, without enduring the humiliation of a first date, which I'll fail at because I'll never in a million years figure out how to reach this level of pretty again.

But in all seriousness, I wanted to take aim for a good guy, and you're it. I like the fact you're in the Navy. I like the fact that you work with disenfranchised kids. I think you're a nice man. Hell, I don't even care if that's not your real picture because responsible men do it for me. Of course, in my world they're like mythical unicorns, they just don't exist, at least not for me. But the dream of a responsible man makes my panties damp. See I can say this safely, 'cause you're not going to respond, and I'm never going to meet you.

So, that's my story, SailorBoy69. Just know that out there in this big bad world a woman thinks you're pretty exceptional, except for the atrocious cyber name you've given yourself. Now, if you have a thought of responding, for God's sake don't. Re-

member, it's me. I have a kid, two jobs, and I'll look like crap, and you'll ruin the fantasy.

—Signed, So Not Mary Poppins

Dex considered his problem. It wasn't just that he wanted to respond to the woman, it was the fact that she was responding to someone who wasn't him. He, Dexter Anthony Evans, had not created this profile.

"Yeah, but it's you," he admonished himself. Clint had done an exceptional job writing up his online resume. He'd even found a formal picture of him in his dress whites that was fairly recent. Dex shouldn't be surprised that Clint had every detail right about him, after all, if Dex wanted to spend eight hours, he could compile an equally comprehensive profile on Clint Archer. The only fake thing had been the initial e-mail to Mary Poppins.

He took another swallow of his Dos Equis beer and really thought it through. He hadn't felt this punch of interest in years. Even if it had started out as a joke, he had to follow through. Now he had to figure out a way to keep her from going into hiding when he responded. Because let's face it, his response was going to panic the hell out of her.

Dex paced the length of his living room. He was going to have to use finesse. His e-mail would need just the right tone, so she didn't run and hide. She was definitely a runner, he grinned. It was his job to coax her out to play. He wanted to get her to agree to meet in person, and these first few back and forths were the way to make it happen. This was going to be fun.

Dinner was four hours ago, he needed some brain food before he started his composition. It needed to be funny, he knew that. He could be funny, but seriously, she took the cake. He perused the contents of his fridge. Yogurt and fresh cherries would be the smart way to go because tomorrow was a training day and he'd just had two beers, but the left over Chinese food was calling his name.

His phone rang as he was snatching the white carton of beef lo mein out of the fridge.

"Evans," he answered.

"We've got a live one," he heard his lieutenant say. "How soon can you report?"

Dex lived in a townhome thirty miles from the base.

"I'm at home," he told Gray. "It all depends on how traffic is on the Five."

"We'll be wheels up as soon as the team gets here. Let's hope the freeway gods are smiling tonight."

The line went dead. Dex turned off his laptop, then swung to his bedroom and pulled out the duffel he kept packed at all times. He toed out of his sandals and tugged on socks and boots. When he went back to the living room, he snagged his laptop and tucked it into the vinyl laptop sleeve and shoved that into the duffel bag and then grabbed his phone, keys, and wallet and headed for the door.

When he got into his jeep, he made a call to his grandfather.

"Dexter, my boy. It's late on a Friday night, shouldn't you be out on a date? After all, you have hundreds of women to choose from."

He laughed. "Thanks for the reminder. I'm so going to get Clint for this."

"According to your grandmother, he did you a favor. She's been wanting great-grandbabies for a couple of years now."

"That's news to me. I would have thought all those summers having me foisted on you was enough."

"You and your brother were back east when you were really young. She says she didn't get a proper grandbaby fix. You're her hope, and you've been letting her down."

Dex snorted. But it got him thinking. His grandmother was really nurturing, he could see where she would want a great-grandchild.

"Are you listening to me?" his grandfather asked.

"What?" Dex asked as he pulled onto the freeway.

"I asked if you were done going through all the e-mails."

"Got just one to go. But right now, I'm headed outta town for a bit."

"Sounded like you were on the road, Kiddo."

Dex grinned again. It killed him that at six-foot-three and two hundred and twenty pounds, he could be called Kiddo. "You guessed it."

"Sorry to hear you're going to miss our tee time on Sunday. I went to the driving range today. I was killing it. You were going to lose money."

"What are you talking about? I always lose money. Old Man, you're a hustler." He was too. The man had somehow manipulated his handicap so he could consistently shoot below it. The two of them would bet a couple of bucks a hole, and Dex would end up owing a ton by the end of the day.

"I promise to teach you all of my secrets before I die," his grandfather's voice promised through the jeep's speaker.

"Bullshit, I want to know your secrets now so I can beat your ass," Dex said without heat.

Martin Evans laughed. "Not going to happen Kiddo. Are you headed to the base?"

"Got it in one," Dex affirmed.

Martin was retired Navy, he'd been stationed all over the world, but his last assignment had been at the 32nd Street Naval Station in San Diego. He was a retired master chief petty officer. In Dex's opinion, nothing could be better than following in his grandfather's footsteps.

"You going wheel's up?"

"Yep."

"I'll have Andrea take care of your plants. They should just be coming back to life about the time you come back."

That was no lie. His young cousin had a green thumb.

"Thanks, Gramps. Give my love to Gram."

"Always. Be safe."

"You know it."

* * *

Lieutenant Grayson Tyler looked grim, which wasn't normal. Even before the most trying assignments, he would be calm and easy when talking to the six men on his SEAL team. If Dexter had to guess, his demeanor had to do with the two men in suits standing near Captain Hale in the back of the briefing room.

"We're heading to Alexandria, Egypt. The situation is fluid," Gray told his men.

Aiden O'Malley, the second in command, caught Dex's eye. Fluid was code for fucked up.

"The American ambassador's daughter, son-in-law, and two small children are missing," Gray continued. "The Anders' family was boating in the Mediterranean. The yacht they were on was found abandoned, except for the bodies of the four marines who had been assigned to guard them. The abandoned yacht with the dead bodies was found five hours ago, and we were informed two hours ago. The head of Egypt's special forces has taken point on this. Our role is an advisory capacity only."

Dex felt his teammates tense up. No wonder Gray looked grim. Shit, he must be pissed. Marines were dead, and they were sending them in as advisors? What kind of happy horse-shit was this?

"Any ransom demands? Anybody taking credit for their disappearance?" Aiden asked.

"No. But terrorist threats have been significant in that region, which is why they had the marines with them," Gray answered.

"Are you telling me that no bad guys were killed and found on the yacht, and there were four marines?" Dex asked.

Gray turned to the suits, and they shook their heads. Gray turned to the team. "According to 777," he said referring to Egypt's special forces, "there were no bodies other than the marines and a couple of crew members."

"You've got to be shitting me," Dalton Leeds said. All the SEALs nodded.

"The American Military police are expected to have gone over the yacht by the time we get there. They'll determine if there were tangos whose bodies were taken off the yacht."

Dex knew immediately that having the MP's playing in the sandbox along with the 777 was what helped make the mission 'fluid.'

Captain Hale stepped forward and stood next to Gray. "Men, I know I can count on you and your lieutenant to do the right thing."

Gray gave the team an imperceptible nod.

Dex and the others got it. These were Americans who were likely held by terrorists. They were going to be rescued by SEALs. To hell with the advisory role. It was just a matter of finding out where they were located.

Gray looked at his team. "Gentlemen, wheels up in ten."

He went to go talk to the captain and the suits.

* * *

They were fifty-five minutes from touching down at the newly minted Mohammed Naguib Military Base west of Alexandria when Dex called Aiden and Gray over to him. He had his computer up.

"We've got a major curve ball," Dex told his commander.

"Spill it."

He pointed to a picture of a jeweled dagger on his computer screen. "Stolen Egyptian artifacts. This one from Cairo's Museum of Antiquities."

"What about it?" Aiden asked.

"There's currently an on-line auction for it. It's up to three-hundred and fifty thousand USD. Considering the fact that it is supposed to be on tour in Asia at the moment, that's pretty significant."

"Go on," Gray said.

"CIA has been tracing all incoming and outgoing e-mails to the US embassy in Cairo. They found a fishy one that led to this auction. It came from Anders' computer," Dex said, referring to the ambassador's son-in-law who had been on the yacht.

"That's more than significant. That gives us one more reason why the family could be missing," Aiden said.

"This could be an inside job," Gray agreed.

It made Dex sick to his stomach to think that the marines could have been killed by the very people they had been sent to guard. But...

"Why would he abandon everything? He has a pretty sweet deal just selling off artifacts and living a life that allows him to vacation on yachts?" Dex asked.

"Still has to live with his father-in-law" Aiden pointed out.

"Have they passed this information onto the US Army Military Police?" Gray questioned.

"Yes. They're watching the auction. They want to see how the money would be paid out, and then they can track him."

Aiden and Gray nodded their heads.

The plane began its descent and went back to their seats. Dex continued to monitor his computer for as long as he could. By the time they set down, Washington DC had sent Dex and the MPs rundowns on the three main e-mail contacts of Anders.

"Shit," Dex muttered. Anders was in deep.

He closed his computer and followed the others off the plane. The heat hit him hard as he disembarked.

"I wanted to work on my tan." Wyatt Leeds grinned.

Dex saw Hunter roll his eyes a second before he donned his sunglasses. The tarmac wavered in front of him from the heat roiling off the ground.

"Welcome," a man in an Egyptian uniform said formally to Dex and the others. "We have quarters set up for you."

"I was told that Captain Adams would be here," Gray said referring to the head MP handling the investigation.

"He's been detained. I am Major Mohammed Farouk. I will be coordinating your stay here on base."

"Thank you," Gray said with a nod. "These are my men. This is my second-in-command Senior Chief Aiden O'Malley. Then you have Dalton Sullivan, Wyatt Leeds, Griffin Porter, Hunter Diaz and my computer specialist, Dexter Evans."

The major acknowledged them with a stiff nod, then pointed to a truck. They loaded up and were soon in front of a building that had been recently built. The base had just officially opened and was considered to be the gem of the Middle East. He grinned when they got inside, it did his heart good to know that a barracks was a barracks, even if it was supposed to be a jewel.

"You've arrived in time for our midday meal. It will be in a half hour," the major informed Gray. "My man will come and escort you to the dining hall in twenty minutes." He turned and left.

"Get situated. I'm going to see what's keeping Adams and maybe we can have some answers by the time we've eaten," Gray told them.

Dex dumped his shit on one of the bunks and immediately pulled out his laptop. "Lieutenant," he called Gray over. "I need to show you some intel that came in right before we landed."

Aiden followed Gray over to Dex's bunk. "Whatchya got?" Gray asked.

"Anders has actually been playing footsy with Taruk El Mahdy, along with two big time collectors."

"El Mahdy? Is he out of his goddamn mind?" Aiden demanded. "He's number three on the US terrorist watch list!"

"It's not El Mahdy directly, it's his cousin out of Tangiers. According to the guys at Langley, there is no doubt that he's a conduit to El Mahdy. Everything has been encrypted. They're working on getting the e-mail content, but they don't know when they'll get it decrypted."

"And the collectors?" Gray asked.

"One's out of London, the other's out of Hong Kong. The encryption on their e-mails have been easy to break. They found out that Anders has been selling artifacts for damn near the entire four years his father-in-law, Ambassador Letterman, has been stationed in Egypt."

Dex wasn't surprised to see the looks of disgust on Aiden and Gray's faces. It was the same thing he was feeling. Asshole had a fan-fucking-tastic life with a beautiful wife and two daughters and was a greedy, grasping bastard who was risking the lives of his family. Plus, he was getting into bed with one of the evilest assholes in the world. The whole thing made Dex want to punch a wall.

"Dex, did you hear me?"

"What?" He needed to keep his shit sorted.

"I asked if they've found any connection to the ambassador."

"Nada so far, but they're continuing to look," Dex answered.

"Gray!" Hunter called from near the entrance of the barracks. Their heads turned and saw that one of the Egyptian soldiers had arrived. He was standing at attention.

"Come on everyone. Time to eat," Gray called out.

* * *

Captain Adams arrived ten minutes after they returned to the barracks. He was one of those wiry men who seemed to vibrate with energy. His gaze missed nothing during the introductions, and he zeroed in on Dex.

"Did you get the intel from DC?" he demanded immediately.

"Yep, I briefed my lieutenant and second-in-command."

"My guy tried to tell me what was going on when I was driving here, but he kept cutting out. I think I got the gist, and if I did, it changes everything. Let's go over it, and I'll tell you what I found out from my inspection of the yacht. It wasn't good."

Dex laid out everything the suits in Washington, DC had given him. Then it was Adams' turn to share.

"Two of the marines were shot point blank in the interior family area. They didn't have their weapons drawn. It's my assessment they were the first two assassinated. The third marine, Sergeant Keith was up on the bridge when things went south. Blood splatter showed that he was coming down the stairs when he was shot in the head. Last, Corporal Hernandez was below deck. His weapon was drawn as well, no shots. His body landed on top of an interrupted fucking game of fucking Candyland." With every word, his voice rose.

Nobody said anything for long moments. Finally, Griffin Porter asked, "how old are the daughters?"

"Four and five," Dexter answered.

Again silence.

"The crew?" Gray asked.

"According to the manifest, there should have been five men besides the captain. He's nowhere to be found. Two of the crew were found in the engine room with bullets in their brains, the rest are gone."

"So, this was definitely an inside job," Adams stated.

"Weren't there security cameras?" Dex asked.

"All of the footage has been pulled."

"That clinches it. It was an inside job," Gray said.

"Are you telling me that Anders allowed a man to be shot and bleed out in front of his daughters?" Gray said slowly and quietly.

"Everything points to this being an inside job. I hope to God that a father would have protected his girls, but I don't think he did," Adams answered.

The rage Dex had felt before that Anders would risk his wife and daughters to sell antiquities morphed into something he could barely contain. He pictured Hernandez sitting cross-legged playing the children's game with the two little girls and then blood spraying, and the girls screaming.

"Is he doing this supposed kidnapping with or without El Mahdy's help?" Aiden asked Adams.

"He couldn't have pulled this off without El Mahdy. The terrorist isn't a bidder, he's a supplier." The Captain's eyes glittered with anger. "Anders is acting as a middle man for El Mahdy."

Dex nodded. The captain was right, it made perfect sense.

"Now we just have to do the investigating to prove it," Adams said. "To me, this looks more like an investigation than a SEAL team operation at this point."

"Until we get called home, we're staying," Gray said quietly. All his men's heads nodded in agreement.

Adams eventually nodded. It was clear he wasn't pleased, but he was going to deal with it.

CHAPTER TWO

"I really want a cheeseburger. Maybe pizza. How about a steak?" Dalton said to no one in particular.

"This sitting around and watching Dex play on his computer is boring as shit," Wyatt complained. "How long is this going to take? We've been here eight days."

Dex looked around at the men who had just come out of the showers. They had spent the last four hours doing physical training in the camp gym, then donned fifty-pound backpacks and ran ten miles in the desert heat. Dex had done the gym time with them but had opted out of the run so that he could coordinate with Langley, but they didn't have anything new. He agreed with Wyatt, it was boring waiting for something to happen. The only thing that had kept him occupied, besides the physical training, had been Mary Poppins. He reread his e-mail one last time. It had only taken five days and nine fucking drafts to get it right.

Dear SNMP,

So, you don't consider yourself Mary Poppins? Well, I've got to call you something for now, so how about Poppy until you tell me your real name? Please don't call me SailorBoy, Boy, Sailor, Popeye, or anything else but my name, which is Dex.

Yep, you looked pretty damn good in the photo, but that's not the reason I'm responding, so you don't need to go buy more product. Buckle-up, Buttercup, your appeal is that you made me laugh. A lot. Now that I told you that, I figure you're probably going to be all paranoid and try to hire a joke writer. I think they're all on strike, so don't bother trying to find one. What's more, your paranoia is part of your charm.

I know you told me not to respond, but Poppy, you made it impossible not to. You told me what does it for you, so let me return the favor. I liked your attitude. I liked your self-deprecation, I liked that your number one priority was your son. Your smile was just the cherry on top.

I have a job that gives me some flexibility in time, but then there are days when I have to be away at a moment's notice. Not real conducive to a relationship, but some of my friends have made it work in a big way.

In an effort to reassure you, since you're all about your kid and responsibility, I'm not looking for a hook-up. But let me guess, that's going to have you running for the hills, right? But be honest, if I said I was looking for a one night stand you would have run, if I said I was looking for something deeper, you were going to run. No matter what, you were going to run because after all, you told me not to respond.

*But I read between the lines. You've got guts. Hell, you've got
balls! So, I'm throwing down.*
Respond.
You were bold once, do it again.
I dare you.
- Dex

He logged onto his personal e-mail and pressed send.

"Dammit, this is boring, with a capital 'B!' I want to see
some action," Wyatt damn near shouted. That took Dex out
of his trance, and he looked up and laughed, he was no longer
in Poppyland, he was back with his team in Egypt. Well almost. He surely hoped his dare would work.

"You always want action." Griffin Porter grinned at Wyatt.

"Griff, it's not cool making fun of the guy who hasn't had
a date in two months. You have Miranda, something tells me
you get plenty of action."

Griffin didn't say anything, but the smile that spread
across his face said it all.

Wyatt groaned. "I guess I need to start taking the train."

Gray walked in. "If we're talking about the train, we must
be talking about Miranda. How is she doing, Griff?"

"She's fine. Kicking ass and taking names. Said she had
lunch with Aiden's woman."

Aiden's head shot up from where he was cleaning his
weapon. He grinned. "Evie and Miranda had lunch? That's
good." Dex watched as both men's faces relaxed into satisfied
smiles.

"Stop talking about your women!" Wyatt demanded. "Dex or Gray, tell me something is going to start happening here. It's been over a week."

Dex looked at Wyatt, who was the youngest of the group and still hadn't learned patience.

"Adams is due to arrive any minute," Gray announced. "He's bringing two of his men."

"Well hot damn." Wyatt sat forward on his bunk. "Ever since the news people got involved, I thought this mission was going to be a bust."

The ambassador had made his family's disappearance into a media circus, despite the warnings he'd received from the US government and the military police. However, no mention of missing artifacts or El Mahdy had been made.

Gray's phone rang just as Captain Adams walked into the barracks along with two MPs who towered over him. Gray gave a chin tilt to Aiden to take over talking to the military police while he took his phone call.

"Captain, we've set up a conference area over here." Aiden indicated three tables they'd shoved together near the back of the large room. Everybody sat down and introduced themselves.

"It sounds like your team has been busy," Aiden said to the captain.

"Shouldn't we wait for Lieutenant Tyler?" the captain asked.

"He'll catch up," Aiden assured him. "What information do you have for us?"

"The latest artifacts didn't come from Egypt, so it took a little longer to track down," Adams said. "It was almost an entire room of the Syrian state museum. We're talking Greco-Roman busts, weapons, and jewelry."

"What kind of bids are they getting?" Hunter asked.

"In total, this will be well over two hundred million."

Dalton whistled.

"I thought all of the Syrian artifacts were going to be captured by ISIS," Griffin said.

"They were," Adams explained. "We've finally decrypted the e-mails between Anders and El Mahdy's cousin. It was El Mahdy's men who stole the Syrian artifacts. Anders is the seller."

"I don't get it, why would they kidnap the family? Don't they need Anders kept in place?" Hunter asked.

"Langley said that they knew there was an antiquities operation going on close to the embassy," Dex said. "They were closing in." Dex turned to Adams. "I've been crunching through the e-mails too. Have you noticed some of the overlap going from Bill Anders account and the Protocol Officer's account?"

"So?" Adams said. "He's just using his other named account and his titled account."

"Noreen Anders, the Ambassador's daughter, is the protocol officer," Dex explained slowly.

Adams looked at him incredulously. "You can't mean she's involved. This is him. He's the bad guy in all of this. El-

Mahdy made a deal with Anders to get him off that boat and out of harm's way before the CIA closed in on him."

"Can Anders keep doing what he's doing from someplace else?" Dalton asked.

"He's got four years of contacts, he should," Dex answered.

"So, he hasn't been kidnapped, he's basically run off with his fucking business partner," Aiden said with loathing.

"But he's still in the hands of El Mahdy, and his father-in-law has the international community raising hell about their disappearance," Adams said.

"Aiden. Dex. We have a mission to plan," Gray clipped out as he headed towards them.

Dex looked up and saw that Gray was already in mission-mode.

"What are you talking about?" Adams demanded. "We're still investigating things. There is no mission."

"Captain Adams, I have to ask you to leave, this is classified."

Dex watched as Adams clenched and unclenched his fists, it was clear he was not happy about this turn of events.

"Lieutenant," he said using Gray's lower rank, "I am in charge of this investigation."

"You are still in charge of the investigation. And *I* am in charge of my men. I appreciate your valuable input. It will be noted in my report to command. As of right now, we have different orders that require me to brief them privately. I'm sure you understand."

Adams took a deep breath and nodded. He picked up his hat and motioned for his men to follow him as he strode out of the barracks.

"Shit, Gray, what was that all about?" Aiden asked.

"I couldn't risk this getting back to the Marines. They are chomping at the bit to get in on any kind of retaliatory mission. But command wants us to go. Satellite photos show a terrorist camp in the middle of the Tibetsi mountain range. It was blind luck that they found them. It showed three figures with blonde hair, one adult, and two children. We have to go in mean and fast before we lose our advantage."

"Holy hell, that's the wife and daughters," Wyatt breathed out.

"That's command's assessment," Gray agreed.

"Was it on the Chad or Libyan side of the border?" Hunter asked.

"How in the hell have you even heard of some mountain range called the Betsey mountains, let alone know they are in Chad?" Wyatt asked Hunter.

"I read books from time to time, you should try it," Hunter said dryly.

"It's on the Libyan side. Barely," Gray answered.

Dex logged into the secure server and found photos had been downloaded to him. He twirled his laptop around so his team could see them.

Dex clicked through the eighteen photos, pausing as his teammates assessed and made comments, or asked him to zoom in. After forty-five minutes, they were done.

"Okay, so we have a landing point fifteen clicks away without being seen or heard," Gray surmised. "Based on the number of tents and activity, we have at minimum, thirteen targets. All the Anders are blonde, and so far, we've only had eyes on the girls and mother. Our plan will be to take out all of the targets, acquire the Anders family and call in the helicopters for a pick-up to take us back to Egypt."

Dex looked around the table at his team. Everyone was grinning at the same thing. Gray had managed to distill a detailed plan to kill the world's third most dangerous terrorist and rescue four hostages into four sentences.

"What?" Gray asked.

"Nothing. I just wonder what you'd tell us to do on D-Day?" Hunter said.

"That's easy. I'd say, 'take the damn beach.'" Gray grinned.

"When do we go out?" Aiden asked.

"Just have to call for our ride," Gray answered as he picked up his phone.

* * *

It was three o'clock in the morning. The moon was waning, so they didn't have a lot of light, which was perfect. They had their night vision goggles. They had memorized the layout of the camp. Seven tents. Four clustered together, one well away from the others to the west, and two clustered together on the east. They had it planned. Three men would take the west side of the camp, four would take the east. There were three trucks parked haphazardly, they would be used for cover.

They had their coms so they could communicate.

"Guard sleeping in front of the far west tent," Aiden whispered. Dex saw the man was holding an AK47 across his lap, and his head was resting on his chest.

"Guard on eastern tent eliminated," Hunter whispered.

"Going in," Griffin said even softer. Dex knew that meant he was slipping into one of the two tents.

Aiden gave Dex the nod, and he ghosted behind the sleeping guard, putting his hand over the man's mouth as he yanked the rifle out of his hand. Then Dex pulled out his knife and punched it into the man's heart holding him tight until he went slack.

"Guard on western tent dead," Aiden whispered.

Dex followed Dalton as they took the larger of the two tents. Aiden headed to the smaller tent. Slipping in silently, Dex was assaulted by the smell of garlic and body odor. Dex and Dalton were on the two inhabitants before they could roll over. Once assured that they were targets, they were easily dispatched.

"Two down," Dalton whispered.

"Two more down," Aiden panted through his mic. He sounded out of breath. Dammit! Dex prayed there wasn't a problem.

"One more down at east tent," Gray said softly. "No sign of any of the Anders. Meet up at the south side of tents."

"Affirmative," Aiden growled. Dalton gave Dex a look, and they headed out of the tent searching for Aiden. He moved toward them. Slowly.

Dammit!

Dex searched him and finally saw it. Aiden was favoring his left side.

"How bad?" Dex asked.

"I'm a go," Aiden said through gritted teeth.

Dex looked at Aiden and took him at his word. He wouldn't risk their mission for pride.

When they met up with Gray and the others, they looked at the remaining tents. There was one that was significantly larger than the others with trucks parked in front of the entrance.

"We'll start there. Aiden sit this out—"

Seven sets of eyes turned to the tent on the left of the large one. A beam of light had just flashed across the interior.

"Dex, you're with me," Gray said. "We're going to shut this shit down. Hunter and Wyatt take the southeast tent. Griff and Dalton take the northwest. Then we're all going to take the large one. That has to be the Anders' location. Aiden, keep an overall watch. Notify us if there is a problem."

With one forward motion, Gray sent his men into silent action. Dex noted that the flashlight kept bobbing around the tent. Whoever had control of it, sure wasn't being careful. Maybe they thought they didn't have to worry since it was three in the morning. But in his opinion, they were stupid. That just meant they needed to be more careful because stupid meant that they were dealing with even more of a wildcard.

Gray took the right side of the tent, and Dex took the left. As he came to the tent, he heard muffled sounds. His Arabic wasn't all that great. Hopefully, Gray would be able to understand what was being said. But as he got closer, he realized English was being spoken.

"Get away from me." It was a man's voice.

"Please, Bill, get up. You've got to get up. I have a plan." It was a woman's voice.

It had to be the Mrs. Anders.

"Bitch, go back to El Mahdy."

"I can't. He's an animal. He's not like he was in Cairo. It's all different now."

"What the fuck did you expect? He's a fucking terrorist!" the man rasped out. "What are you doing, Noreen?"

"I'm trying to cut the ropes."

"I can't walk. I don't think I could stand, let alone walk. Where are the girls?"

"They're asleep in a tent with the other two women in the camp. I gave them the last of my Ambien. They'll sleep until morning. You have to help me get the girls and get one of the trucks."

"They'll kill us all. Our only hope is me trading the account passwords for Lottie and Clara's safe passage out of this hell-hole."

"You should never have stuck your nose in my business!"

"What the fuck are you talking about? If I hadn't of gotten the bank account information, we would be fucked right now, it's the only leverage we have with your boyfriend." He said the last word with disdain. "I pray to God we can trade them for our daughter's lives."

"What about me?" the woman's voice trembled.

"You literally made your bed, you can lie in it."

"Taruk will never let the girls go. He plans to raise them and marry them off when they turn thirteen."

"He won't if he wants the money out of the accounts."

There was a click on Dex's earpiece. "The targets in the northwest tent are eliminated," Griff reported.

"Got a situation in our tent," Hunter said.

"Sleeping women and children?" Gray asked.

"Affirmative."

"Aiden," Gray bit out.

"I'm on it," Aiden quickly replied.

"The rest of you surround the main tent. Dex and I have a situation. We found the husband and wife. The husband is injured. The rest of the targets, including El Mahdy, are in the main tent. Take them out."

"Turn off the goddamn flashlight!" Anders damn near shouted. What the hell was he thinking, Dex wondered. The last thing he needed to do was wake up the terrorists.

"I can't see, I'll cut you," Noreen responded.

As one, Dex and Gray entered the tent.

"Quiet. Not one more word," Gray commanded. "He's right, shut off the flashlight."

The bright light fell onto the dirt and illuminated the bloodied, beaten, and naked man who had his wrists tied to his ankles behind his back. It was clear he had been tortured.

Dex breathed a mental sigh of relief when the woman didn't speak.

"We're going to get you out of here," Gray said. "Nod if you understand."

She nodded.

Dex pulled out his knife and made quick work of the ropes holding the man. "Don't move. When you move it's going to hurt like a motherfucker," Dex warned him. He grabbed the man's left arm and slowly rotated his shoulder forward, at the same time massaging his wrist. He gave a low howl of pain.

Noreen knelt, touching his other shoulder, beginning to gently knead.

"Don't fucking touch me!" Dex saw the desperate pain the man was in, but it was clear he would endure the fires of hell before he would let his wife lay hands on him.

"I didn't know they would do this to you, Bill. Please let me help you."

"Get them ready to go, I'm with the others," Gray said as he left the tent.

A shot rang out. Then the unmistakable sound of an AK47 rent the night.

A man shrieked.

Dex went to Bill's legs, assessing as he straightened them. They weren't broken, but he would definitely need help walking. Depending on the situation, Dex figured it might be easier to just carry him.

More gunfire.

"Keep them away from that tent!" Hunter yelled into his mic.

"I've got it covered," Aiden said calmly.

Dex smiled grimly. It didn't matter if he was injured and alone, Aiden O'Malley would make sure nothing and no one would get to those girls.

Spurts of gunfire sounded, this time closer to their tent. Dex crouched and moved to the entrance, holding his assault rifle up and ready. He peeked out and saw a man behind one of the trucks.

The man was making his way toward Dex's location. He lifted his arm throwing something at the same time that Dex shot him in the head. In an instant, Dex estimated the distance between the truck and the tent and realized they were going to be hit hard with debris.

"Down!" he shouted, as he lunged at the Anders, tackling them. Something big and sharp careened through the side of the canvass.

"Ahhhhhh," Bill Anders shrieked. Warm wet covered Dex's hand.

Fuck! It was blood. A lot of blood. He pushed up and saw that he might have successfully covered the couple's heads, but Bill Anders' legs had been left unprotected. Part of the truck's windshield was embedded in the man's upper thigh, near his groin. He was spurting blood. His femoral artery was shooting blood like a geyser.

"Report." It was Gray.

"Anders is hit. It's bad," Dex said into his mic as he moved his hand over Anders' leg. He assessed the situation.

"Miz Anders, I need your help. I'm going to try to stem the bleeding, you need to remove the glass."

Dex reached into the wound on his thigh, finding the bleeder. Mrs. Anders wasn't moving.

"Mrs. Anders!" He swung his head around and found the woman staring at her husband. She didn't seem to in shock, she just wasn't helping.

"Goddammit, pull out the glass."

She shook her head.

Blood pulsed through his fingers. He needed to stop it, but he couldn't apply any sort of tourniquet with the glass in his way. "Mrs. Anders, I need your help."

Suddenly, she sprang forward, shoving herself in her husband's face.

"You're going to die, Bill. Tell me the passwords."

Dex watched as Bill spit saliva and blood into his wife's face. "Fuck you, Noreen," he gasped.

"Tell me," she screeched.

"He won't be able to tell you shit, if you let him die," Dex ground out. "Pull out the glass."

"Bill, if you want help, you'll tell me the passwords," she hissed at her husband.

Dex stared in amazement at the woman who had a mixture of blood and spittle dripping down her face. Was she crazy?

"Lady, he's going to die!"

"Then he better answer quick!"

Bill turned to Dex. "Save my daughters."

"Don't you dare die," the woman yelled.

"Coming in," Gray said through the earpiece. Dex felt a gust of night air as the tent opened and Gray knelt beside him. He had a tourniquet ready. Dex drew out the glass, and Gray applied it. But it was too late. The blood had stopped pumping.

Dex put his hand over the man's open eyes and closed them.

"What are you doing? Stop that!" Mrs. Anders cried.

"I'm sorry, Ma'am," Gray said. "He's dead. We need to get you and your daughters back home."

"He can't be dead. I need the passwords!"

Her shrill voice made Dex wince.

"Is she for real?" Gray asked Dex.

He gave a short nod, then asked. "What's the status?"

"We've taken out everyone but the women. Including El Mahdy."

Behind him, he heard a thud. He turned in time to see Mrs. Anders hitting her husband's corpse. The woman was fucked in the head.

"Lady, what are you doing?" Gray demanded.

"He left me with nothing!" she wailed.

"What about your daughters? Aren't you going to ask about them?" Dex demanded

Her hands went limp against the man's naked body. Her eyes slid to Gray, and even in the darkness, Dex could see the insincerity. "Are Lottie and Clara okay?" she whispered. "I'd die if something bad happened to them."

Gray took his time answering. Finally, he said, his voice laced with contempt, "they're fine." He turned to Dex. "Aiden called for an evac. They should be here within the hour."

Dex nodded. He heard another thud behind him as she hit her husband's body one last time.

CHAPTER THREE

Dex,

So, you don't think that SailorBoy and Poppy would make a cute couple, huh? I don't know, think about it. We could get matching tattoos. We could get license plates with each other's handles. I really think you should consider it.

No?

Okay. But if you insist on daring me, then expect to get every single piece of Popeye or Aqua man memorabilia that I can find on E-Bay.

I didn't realize you were cocky. I'm not sure how I feel about that. It's kind of like arrogant, which can be a turn-off. But you were so darned amusing, and nice, so here I am drinking a glass of wine and typing. Yep, almost as bad as drinking and texting.

Damn! I think I'm in over my head.

Look, I appreciate hearing that you have friends who've made it for the long haul despite the time apart, but they must have something really special. I don't think I'm built for special. I'm ordinary and complicated. Mundane even.

Don't take this as a challenge, just as the truth. Didn't other women respond to you? I'm sure there are far more suitable matches.

-Poppy

It had taken five days to get home after the mission was completed. Five days where Dex had the dichotomy of Noreen Anders and Poppy rolling around in his head. Thank God, she had responded, it helped wash out the vile memories of the repugnant mother.

After thirty, he had lost count of how many times he read Poppy's response. It had helped to soothe him when he remembered the look on little Clara Anders' face when she had sought comfort from her mother and gotten slapped in return.

Even now, it enraged him to think about it, and was why concentrating on Poppy and the here and now was so important.

As soon as they'd docked, he'd gotten the hell out of there damn near as quickly as Aiden and Griff. Hell, Dalton still had his mouth open to give him shit about his abrupt departure, but the door had closed too fast.

He'd composed his response to Poppy while he'd been on the carrier, but he wanted to be in the right headspace so that he could handle her next reply. What's more, if she didn't send an e-mail, he wanted to be in San Diego so he could accidentally 'run into her.' He'd prefer not to have to hack the dating site, but he'd be damned if he wouldn't meet this woman.

It was nine o'clock in the evening when he hit his town-home. As soon as he turned on the lights, he chuckled. Not only had Andrea watered his plants, he saw that she had added new ones to his ever-expanding greenhouse. It was her way of making sure that she had reasons to drop by. He prayed that none of them were 'killing plants.' Sometimes she would purchase exotics that he couldn't keep alive if his life depended on it. Those she would take home and triage and not bring back. However, a couple she'd told him never did come back to life.

He dumped his duffle in the living room and pulled out his laptop and booted it up. He went to the fridge to see what else Andrea might have waiting for him.

Score!

There was some Yoo-hoo that wasn't expired. Seriously, the girl spoiled him. He knew the money came from Gramps, but the thought was from his young cousin.

What a gem.

He opened one yellow bottle and took a swig, and snagged a second to take to the couch.

Now.

Finally.

At last.

"Let's hope this does this trick," he said to himself.

Poppy,

I'm thirty-two years old. You know that from my profile. I'm old enough to know my own mind and know what and who is suitable. I think you're funny, complex, and a little bit neurotic. Sorry, Poppy, it fits, and on you Baby, it's sexy as hell.

All in all, I would say you suit me down to my bones.

Tell me what you need from me to keep this correspondence going. What do I have to say? What do I have to do, to make you take a chance on meeting me? I can e-mail over my Navy performance evaluations. Would you like my grandmother to send a letter of recommendation? It might be a little bit biased. What do I need to do, because Poppy, you need to know, I'm interested in the long game.

-Dex

Fuck! He sure as hell hoped he was reading her right. But every instinct told him that he needed to keep pushing. That if he backed down, she would just stop responding. Pray God he was right.

He sucked down the second bottle of Yoo-hoo, and put his laptop on the coffee table and headed for the shower. He needed one.

* * *

"Get a move on!" Kenna shouted up the stairs. Seriously, that boy had only two speeds lightning or dawdle. Mornings were always dawdle.

"I can't find my socks."

"Austin, there are eighteen pairs of socks in your drawer, what are you talking about?" Kenna demanded as she headed up the stairs.

"They're my lucky socks." She heard him say from his room. "I have a wrestling match today. I need my lucky socks."

"No such thing. You win or lose based on your performance," she said as she rounded the corner into his room where he was pawing through his sock drawer.

"Found 'em," he grinned up at her as he waved them up in triumph, before shoving them into his gym bag. Kenna shook her head. As he passed her in the doorway, Austin brushed the charm bracelet on her wrist. The one that had the gold four leaf clover charm her dad had given her on her sixteenth birthday. She wore it every day and even tucked it into her pants pocket when she was working.

"So, Mom, I wonder where I got my superstitious nature from?" He smirked.

"What a smartass."

"Yeah, but I'm your smartass."

That he was. What was she going to do with him?

"Come on, get the lead out. I'm going to be late for school," he yelled from the hallway. She stifled a laugh. Was it normal for a mother to get such a kick out of their kid? Kenna shook her head and headed down the stairs where Austin was waiting for her with a grin on his face. He even knew he was entertaining. They grinned at one another and headed out to the car.

She swung by Denny's house and picked him up, and then dropped the two teenagers off at the high school. Kenna couldn't believe that she actually had a son in high school. How in the hell had that happened? She was only thirty-two. Oh yeah, she'd gotten knocked up when *she* was in high school. She looked at her son's broad shoulders and wondered if she needed to have *another* talk with him about safe sex, or if last week's talk was enough.

She had just enough time to drive through Starbucks for a skinny latte before her shift started. Kenna mentally geared up for the day. She knew some of the people she would be seeing. Mr. Renfew, Laurie, and Harold would be in for their chemo treatments today. She winced when she thought about Harold. It was Thursday so his son would be bringing him in. That man couldn't catch a clue even if Colonel Mustard was helping him. How in the hell could she convince him she just wasn't interested in going out? Just because he drove a Maserati and had more money than a small nation, he thought he was God's gift to women. Well, he wasn't. He was a jerk. He treated his dad like crap.

After she parked her Honda in the staff parking lot, Kenna hit the lobby of the hospital and made her way to the elevators.

"Hey, Kenna! Wait up."

She held the elevator for her friend.

"Did you get the e-mail I forwarded you? I think he sounded pretty nice, don't you?"

Kenna stopped herself from rolling her eyes.

"I know what you're thinking, but seriously, this guy is different," Jean said as she pressed the up button. "I've been e-mailing him on and off for over a month. I think it's time to meet him. I wanted your opinion of the last e-mail. Didn't you read it?"

"Last night I was at Rosalie's house."

"You're still doing that gig?"

This time Kenna did roll her eyes. "Yes, I'm still doing that gig. I work as Rosalie Randall's personal assistant twice a week and have been doing it for three years. You know that, Jean."

"I thought after your last raise you could quit."

For a doctor, Jean sure wasn't very circumspect. "Lower your voice," Kenna admonished as they exited the elevator.

Jean grimaced. "Sorry. But seriously. Why can't you quit?"

"Two and a half more years and Austin is going to graduate. College costs money."

"Yeah, it does." Jean sighed. "Well okay, read the e-mail tonight. Okay?"

"I will," Kenna promised.

* * *

This was stupid. Why should her palms be sweaty? Kenna stood behind her desk chair, staring at her computer. Austin was asleep. She'd watched his wrestling match. He'd pinned his opponent. He credited his lucky socks.

She should have gone through her personal e-mail yesterday, but she hadn't, she was too busy handling Rosalie's. The woman was a mess and a half. So here she was, almost done with her own.

Almost.

She'd read the one that Jean had forwarded her. She understood why Jean liked him. He said he was an attorney. Jean wanted a guy who was her professional equal, and this guy said he was a partner in a law firm. That would appeal to her. But still, something didn't ring true. Maybe it was the way he mentioned what kind of car he drove. It reminded Kenna too much of Harold's son.

Then there were the four new e-mails responding to her profile. Well, two were new, two were repeats, and one was from SailorBoy69. Jean had questioned why Kenna had even had put herself on CaliSingles, and this was it. Knowing that out there in the cosmos some men found her attractive used to boost her self-esteem. She would read the e-mails, and they would make her smile. SailorBoy69's was the only one she'd ever responded to, and look at the mess she was in.

Kenna was looking at her e-mail in-box like it was full of snakes. She'd told him not to respond. She'd meant it. Hadn't she? Dammit, this panic attack was as bad as the first one she'd had. Shouldn't she be past this?

"Suck it up, Wright, if you had really meant for him not to respond, you wouldn't have sent him an e-mail, let alone two!"

She stomped to her kitchen and opened the top cabinet that housed the wine glasses.

"Dammit. Now he has me drinking alone again. Not a good sign." She poured a glass of red wine. Well, at least it wasn't tequila. The last time she drank tequila was four months ago when she had gotten a call from the sewer sucking slime ball with his latest excuse as to why he couldn't pay child support. Like always, he was out of work, but she would bet any amount of money that he was supporting some stripper's G-string. She hoped that was all, and that he hadn't talked any woman into actually moving in with him because nobody deserved that type of attention.

Great, now she was thinking of Jaden, just the mindset she needed when getting ready to read another e-mail from the first man she'd found attractive since high school. Please say he hadn't dared her again.

"Please, no more dares."

Did she just whimper?

"Pull it together!" She slugged down a swallow of wine and choked.

This was not boding well. It was a sign. She should probably just delete the damn thing and not bother reading it.

Well, you can't very well delete it while you're standing in the kitchen, now can you? Get your ass back into the office.

She started to stomp into the other room, and then remembered that Austin was asleep upstairs. Normally being a mom was great, but when she felt like throwing a hissy fit, it really put a crimp in her style. She placed her glass on the desk, took a deep breath, and opened the e-mail.

Oh holy camoly, she was whimpering. She actually heard a whimper come out of her mouth. He said she suited him down to his bones. It made her want to melt.

With trembling fingers, she touched the rim of her wineglass and kept reading.

"His Grandmother?" she whispered. "His grandmother could write a letter of recommendation?"

She felt tears forming as she smiled. It was a lovely e-mail. It made her feel so warm inside.

He called you neurotic.

She sat up straighter and read that part of the e-mail again. Yep, he'd called her neurotic. But then she smiled. He said she was sexy.

She took another swallow of wine and found herself choking...again.

Fuck nugget!

"Dex, you're a hard man to shake loose."

But did she want to shake him loose? That was the question.

She sat down at the keyboard and started to type.

Dex,

I'm thinking that a letter of recommendation from your grandmother would be soooo slanted in your direction, so I'll pass. But it's good to know she'd write one for you.

Straight up, you're scaring the snot out of me by saying we 'fit.' You don't know me. Okay, the neurotic part is a gimme, but other than that, you don't know me. Here's a little info. My name is Kenna. I shouldn't be telling you that, but you have a grand-mother who loves you, so I think I should tell you my name.

When you said you wanted the correspondence to keep going and you're interested in the long game, it soothed my soul and scared the crap out of me at the same time. Can we start as just friends, and see where things lead? I mean slow. I mean tortoise slow. I mean snail's pace slow. Can you cope with that? Hell, what am I thinking? You probably can't. Which is totally fine. I totally understand.

There is no need for you to respond.

- Kenna aka Poppy

She re-read what she'd typed and bit her nail.

God, she was talking out of both sides of her mouth. Did she want him to respond and go slow, or hope she didn't hear from him again?

"I don't know! God, I'm a basket case." She looked at her empty glass. No help there.

To hell with it. She was who she was. Her mother called her a screwball, and she sure was earning her neurotic stripes. She pressed send, closed her laptop and headed up the stairs.

* * *

Dex had been disappointed when Poppy hadn't immediately responded to his e-mail. Luckily there was more than enough to do to keep him occupied after being gone so long. But the first thing he did after starting the coffee the next morning, was to check his computer, and he did a fist pump.

This time it didn't take him any time at all to come up with a reply. Dex pressed send and then picked up the phone to call his grandfather.

"It's about time you called. I heard via the grapevine you got back yesterday."

Dex shook his head. The old man was totally in the know. "You coming over tonight? Your grandmother misses you."

"I was calling to see about making up that golf game we missed. We've got some down time coming to us. We can leave early today, but that would only give us time for nine holes."

"You going to bring some of your buddies?"

"That was the plan."

"Excellent. But my arthritis is acting up so I might need some extra strokes."

"That's bullshit. You just want to win money. I want to talk to Grandma Helen," Dex demanded. He knew that his grandmother would tell him that his grandfather was just fine.

"She's out in the backyard," his grandfather immediately lied. At least, Dex was pretty damn sure it was a lie.

"See, it's bullshit." Dex loved his grandfather. The man was wily.

"I'll set up a tee time. Is it for four?" Martin asked.

"I'm pretty sure, I'll let you know if anything changes."

He hung up the phone and smiled, then he called Hunter and Gray.

* * *

"Don't hit the ball Son, swing through the ball." Dex's lips twitched when he heard his grandfather say those words to Hunter. How many times had he heard that exact same sentence throughout his adolescence?

Martin Evans threw another golf ball down on the grass. "Tee that up and try again. You'll hit the green for sure this time."

"I can't hit another ball," Hunter protested. He looked at Dex and Gray for assistance. They just grinned at their big friend.

"Suck it up and shoot again," Dex told his friend.

"It's called taking a Mulligan," Martin explained. "You just start over, instead of trying to hit your other shot that went into the rough. Now this time don't try to kill the ball, just swing through it. You have a natural swing. You'll do great."

Dex wasn't surprised in the slightest when Hunter's next ball went straight down the fairway and landed a few feet away from the green. Martin was a natural born teacher.

"Don't get too cocky, you're still going to end up buying the beer tonight," Gray warned him.

"Nonsense. We agreed, Hunter and I would partner against the two of you," Martin said as he grabbed the handle of his portable golf cart. "My arthritis is acting up, so you're going to have to give me two more points for the nine holes. It should be four, but I'm sure Hunter will be able to make up for it."

Dex smothered a grin. His grandfather needed extra handicap points like he needed a hole in the head. The man could outshoot almost any man at the club on the back nine. He and Gray were about to get their asses handed to them.

"Mr. Evans, if your arthritis is acting up, maybe we should have gotten an electric cart so you could have ridden," Hunter suggested.

"Just need to stretch out my muscles, young man. Let's move on ahead and talk about what club you should use when you get up toward the green. Should it be a nine iron, or a wedge? This will take some thought."

Dex purposefully walked slower so that he could talk to Gray. "Have you heard anything about the ambassador's granddaughters? How are they doing?"

"I wanted to ask *you*, how *you* were doing," Gray said. "You and Aiden both seemed to take it pretty hard. Of course, you two were holding the girls in the helicopter."

Dex looked down at the green grass under his feet, so different from the sand that he had trekked over just weeks before. Then he glanced sideways at his friend and boss. "I'll be doing better when you answer my question," he replied.

"I have a friend," Gray paused. "Don't ask me who or how, but suffice it to say they have connections, they told me what is going on."

Dex stopped in the middle of the fairway, watching as his grandfather took out his pitching wedge to explain something to Hunter. "Tell me. Please tell that I'll get to testify against her."

Gray gave him a long look, and Dex realized what that meant. Fuck. The bitch was going to get away with assisting in her husband's death.

"If you can't give me that, at least tell me that she isn't going to have anything to do with raising her daughters."

Dex thought about that moment in the desert when little Clara Anders looked at her mother, begging to know where her daddy was, and that crazy blonde bitch had actually slapped her child and told her to shut up. Before anyone could blink, Dex had picked her up and cuddled her. But Noreen Anders had still been trying to get at her child, so Gray physically restrained her until the helicopters showed up.

"Here's where it stands. Half of the people working the case still think it was Bill Anders who was doing the selling, but the other half belief it was the bitch from hell."

"What about our reports?" Dex asked.

"This is the stuff you and I can't and won't ever know about, but the CIA bureau chief sat down with the ambassador and laid out all they did have, that wouldn't necessarily stand up in a court of law, including our reports. The bureau chief even arranged for a child psychologist to meet with the girls. The ambassador was appalled. Besides the CIA, her father turned on her. The girls were taken from her. Their aunt and uncle will raise them in the US. I checked they're good people."

Of course, Gray checked.

"Tell me something really bad is going to happen to Crazy Noreen," Dex pleaded.

"Crazy Noreen is going to be working with the bureau chief. He's basically turned her into one of his operatives. He's using the threat of your testimony as leverage. He's got her convinced that she could be up on manslaughter charges for not helping you try to save her husband."

That gave Dex a small amount of satisfaction, then he thought of something.

"Her first assignment is working in a village in Somalia for a year, gathering intel about pirates."

"She's the ambassador's blood daughter, and he's okay with this?" Dex hoped to hell he was.

"Yep. He's a good man. He wrote letters of condolences to the four marines families. If she can help stop more of bloodletting, he's for it."

Dex looked at his lieutenant. It was amazing how connected and informed he was. He opened his mouth.

"I told you," Gray said. "Don't ask any questions of who and how I got this information."

Dex shut his mouth and nodded.

"Now, just how hard a time are we going to have beating your granddad?" Gray asked.

"Just get your money out now, we're going down," Dex said.

CHAPTER FOUR

Kenna,

I can be as slow as a herd of snails travelling through peanut butter. See you said slow, and I didn't even make a sexual innuendo because that would have been going fast.

Poppy, I don't know what went on in your past, but if you need slow, and I get to spend some time laughing at my computer screen because of your attitude, I'm all for it. If there ever comes a time where you want to tell me about your past, I'm all ears. (Like a slow-moving elephant going up a hill.)

I lived with Grandma Helen and Grandpa Martin during the summers so it might not be a totally glowing letter of recommendation. She might have thrown in a few zingers about what a handful I was. Hearing that my words soothed your soul made me soar.

I believe in this. Let's keep talking. We're doing the right thing here, Kenna.

- Dex

Kenna threw up her hands.

This shit needed to stop, and it needed to stop now. She bit her lip as she re-read Dex's e-mail. She couldn't even think of him as SailorBoy anymore. He was Dex. She toggled over to the picture that had come with the original e-mail. He was so damned handsome. She stood up and moved across the room then picked up the wedding picture of her parents. Her father had been wearing his dress whites. He had short hair like Dex.

A Navy man.

Honorable.

That was the reason she had responded to him, and she hadn't responded to any other man who had ever e-mailed SNMP.

Admit it, he's hot as hell.

"Down girl!" she said to the empty room.

Kenna only had one lover in her entire life, and she'd had the bad judgement to get knocked up and marry him. All because she had thought he was the most handsome boy in school. She swore to herself years and years ago that if she ever broke up with her vibrator, it was going to be for a homely man. What was she thinking?

He's funny.

He's nice.

He says the nicest things!

"Three good reasons to question whether he's for real, or if you've gone insane!"

Time to nip this in the bud.

She sat down at her computer.

Dex,

I am so sorry I ever responded to you. Thanks for being such a good guy, but this just isn't going to work. You need to find someone else, someone else who will make you laugh. Trust me, you'd get sick of my attitude and neurosis. You need someone with less baggage. Think of it this way, you got away before you had a chance to be burned by the crazy chick. Who needs crazy, right?

Thank you so much for brightening up the last few weeks for me. It meant a lot. I'm shutting down my account now.

Good luck finding someone sane. You deserve it.

- Kenna

Kenna spent the next thirty minutes deleting her profile from the dating website. It should have been faster, but she went to google to make sure that she was doing everything correctly so that every trace would be gone. She'd set up the profile a year and a half ago when she'd been feeling pretty good about herself. Austin had just turned fourteen, and her mom and Rosalie had pushed her to think about dating. So, she had put herself out there. They'd been right, men had been sending her responses ever since she had uploaded.

She got up and took down a wine glass and poured herself a half glass of a nice red. She looked at her fingers, then her hands. For just a moment, she imagined her hands running through Dex's hair. Then she gave a sad laugh.

"Look at them, you don't even have the nails painted," she said to herself.

She took a sip of wine and then, carrying the glass, went to look in the hall mirror. It wasn't a good night to be looking at herself. Her hair was in a messy ponytail, no make-up, and she was tired. Yesterday had been a Rosalie day, so she hadn't gotten much sleep.

Her cell phone vibrated. She always turned off the ringer when Austin was asleep. She saw that it was Rosalie. That was odd. She rarely called her on her days off, and never this late in the evening.

"What's wrong?" Rosalie demanded before Kenna could even say hello.

"What do you mean? Nothing's wrong. Why are you calling?"

"I just got the notification that you took down your profile on CaliSingles. What are you thinking? You were in the top ninety percentile for hits in your age bracket."

"Rosalie, what are you talking about?"

"I had Buddy checking your stats. You actually responded to someone. It was fabulous. What are you doing stopping now?"

"My stats?" Kenna looked at the wine sloshing in her glass and set it on the kitchen counter. "Rosalie, come clean immediately," she demanded of her boss. "What do you mean stats? How did you know I sent someone an e-mail on the site? What did you have your grandson do?"

"I had Buddy purchase the company so we could check up on you. It turned out to be a wonderful investment."

"Let me get this right, you bought a company so you could invade my privacy?" Kenna asked incredulously.

"No. Not at all. Buddy bought it. He had to really fight for it, but he got it. I had him immediately look you up so we could send some matches your way. We wanted to build your confidence. But there was no need. When you first signed up, you were getting plenty of hits on your own. The problem was, you didn't respond to anyone. Kenna, I despaired. For over a year, you did nothing until SailorBoy69. Now you're rejecting him? Seriously, what are you thinking? He's a dreamboat."

"Dreamboat?"

"That's what we would call them in my day, Honey. In my cougar days, I would call him all sorts of other things. Mostly I would just call him up and have my way with him. But now that I hit ninety, I decided to go back to how we talked in the forties. It seems more ladylike."

"Rosalie, I can't keep up," Kenna moaned. She sank back against the kitchen counter and looked at the ceiling. "I can't believe you had Buddy buy a company just so you could see my profile."

"I can't believe you deleted it. You need to re-post it immediately. You also need to continue corresponding with SailorBoy69." Then there was a pause. "Unless he was untoward. Was he unseemly?"

"You mean you didn't read our e-mails?"

"No, Buddy didn't feel comfortable reading the e-mails, he just told me that you two were communicating with one another. Was he a cad?"

"No Rosalie, he was a perfect gentleman."

"Well, in that case, you need to re-post your profile and get back in touch with him. Tonight." Despite the woman's age, her voice was firm.

"Rosalie, I'm going to bed." Kenna's tone was equally firm. "I need to get Austin ready for school early in the morning."

"Kenna, you need to come into the land of the living. Trust me, I had seven husbands. Men are wonderful."

"How can you say that? You had seven husbands. Obviously, things went wrong."

"Nonsense, I only divorced three of them, four died. And they died happy. You're too young to have given up on men. Don't make me take matters into my own hands."

"What do you mean by that?"

"Put your profile back up," Rosalie said ominously.

"No."

"Okay, but don't say I didn't warn you."

Fuck nugget!

* * *

Dex was damn glad that he had set up his computer to ding if an e-mail from "SNMP" should come in. If he hadn't, he might not have been able to download her profile information in time before she deleted it. It was a near thing.

He sat in his dark living room, staring at the glowing screen of his laptop, and started the methodical process of finding out everything there was to know about So Not Mary Poppins aka Kenna. She was Kenna Wright, divorced for nine years. Graduated three years ago with a nursing degree, and was now an oncology nurse. Lots of legal filings showing that her deadbeat of an ex-husband had to have his wages garnished in order to pay child support. But even so, most of the time the great state of California couldn't even find his happy ass to collect the money.

He also found out what her second job was. She was the personal secretary to Rosalie Randall. Hell, he remembered watching that woman's movies. She'd been stunning back in the fifties and sixties. She lived in La Jolla and had an amazing on-line presence, and was in the process of writing her seventh memoir.

Dex didn't do a deep dive on Kenna, he just found out the basics, where she worked and lived. Okay, maybe he stepped over the line a little to find out about the bastard of an ex-husband, but he didn't pull credit reports or DMV records. He was a good boy. But now that he knew where Kenna worked, he had to figure out how to make it seem like an accidental meeting.

He needed to think about this.

When he woke up the next morning to find an e-mail from Rosalie Randall in his in-box, he burst out laughing. Apparently, this was going to be a hell of a lot easier than he had anticipated.

* * *

"You can understand how important this new foundation is going to be. It's imperative it is done right. When Buddy told me that Chief Petty Officer Evans had worked on a program for disadvantaged youth, I thought he would be a perfect candidate to help with this new foundation I'm starting."

Kenna looked at Rosalie as she sat on her verandah, smiling so sweetly butter wouldn't melt in her mouth. Then there was Dex. He was smiling just as broadly. She was ready to blast both of them. But, how could she? Rosalie had brought in five different representatives of missions in San Diego, County and they were all sitting around the table sipping iced tea. Nope, she couldn't have a shit-fit in front of them.

Kenna gritted her teeth then got herself together. Maybe she needed to come from this at a different angle.

"Mr. Evans, are you here representing the Navy?" Kenna asked.

"No Kenna. I'm here in an unofficial capacity. When Rosalie called and introduced herself I was immediately intrigued, I remembered seeing her in movies, in fact, I had quite the crush on her." Dex smiled at Rosalie who was lapping up his compliments like a cat with a bowl of cream.

But no matter how hard Kenna stared at the man, she could see nothing but sincerity radiating from him. It didn't hurt that he had come to the house wearing slacks and a polo shirt that fit his body and accentuated his broad shoulders and strong biceps. Kenna didn't blame Rosalie for her admiration. Hell, she was having a hard time not staring. Then there was the fact that he didn't seem to be bothered by the eight hundred and fifty yippee dogs that ran around the table. Right now, he even had Smooches in his lap!

"I was blown away at the idea of who I would be working with on this team," Dex said looking around the table. Everybody sat up straighter. "All of you have made an impact here in San Diego. Anything I can do to help would be an honor." Then Dex turned to Kenna. "But the cherry on top is Ms. Wright."

Did he just say cherry on top?!

He grinned at her. What a flirt! "Rosalie couldn't sing your praises high enough. She said that I would be working very closely with you to administer the funds. She said that you are her right hand and work as a nurse at Sharp Memorial in the oncology department. Not to mention raising your son all on your own. As soon as you walked out onto the patio, I was looking for angel wings."

Somehow the man had known that she was Poppy because he hadn't been surprised at all when she had walked out. Granted she wasn't all made up and looking like her glamorous picture, but still, her name was Kenna, and she looked close enough that he had to have put it together, and he hadn't acted surprised.

Rosalie must have told him. *Shit!* She needed to nip this in the bud. Like she thought she had three nights ago.

"Rosalie, we still have to coordinate your re-writes with your editor, this project is going to require more time than I have to give. I can only work my normal Wednesdays and Saturdays. I don't think I can co-chair this with Mr. Evans. I'm so sorry."

She shot Rosalie a meaningful glance.

"Buddy has agreed to help me on my memoir and pick-up some of your other duties while you're working on this project," Rosalie piped up.

Buddy grabbed his Monster Energy drink and gulped down a huge swallow, trying to avoid Kenna's glare.

"Buddy, I would have thought with your running such a large online business, you couldn't spare the time," Kenna bit out.

He took a huge bite of his quiche, then pointed to his full mouth and shook his head, indicating he couldn't answer. Coward.

"Then it's settled, you'll have time to work on this. I'm looking forward to it, Ms. Wright," Dex said smoothly.

"Call her Kenna," Rosalie inserted. "She never stands on ceremony." Rosalie turned to the others at the table. "Now let's get down to brass tacks. How does two million sound to start?"

Kenna rolled her eyes.

Dex smothered a laugh.

* * *

Dex had never been in an office with a white shag rug and a pink couch before. Even the desk chair was upholstered in pink. At least the chair he was sitting in was white. He expected to see a white Persian cat slink around his feet at any moment. Well, what else could you expect from someone who had once been a James Bond girl? Rosalie was a character, and she was willing to spend two million dollars to matchmake for her girl. Kenna had to be pretty special, but then he'd already guessed that.

His Poppy was pissed. It looked good on her. She shot daggers at him and Buddy all through the meeting. The looks she had given Rosalie were more gentle. Dex liked that. She'd shown piss and vinegar as well as kindness and compassion. Then there was the way she treated the three women and two men who headed up the San Diego homeless shelters. She'd been terrific with them. She'd ticked off her questions, and figured out immediately which ones were already well-funded, which ones had their shit together, and which ones needed the most help. The woman could probably organize a war zone if need be.

She scheduled walk throughs of the missions next Saturday. Now he was in here cooling his heels while she was taking a break to go to the powder room. He would bet dollars to donuts that she was busting Rosalie and Buddy's chops. Buddy was getting a full-on knock down, whereas Rosalie was getting guilt.

The door of the pink office flew open. A cat sprinted in before Kenna, it was a Siamese, chased by the five teacup poodles who barked madly.

"Out!" The poodles screeched to a halt, butts hitting the rug. They looked at Kenna. She shoved them out the door. The Siamese cat watched with a smug look of superiority. After she shut the door, Kenna turned to Dex and crossed her arms over her chest.

"SailorBoy, you knew it was me. I call foul. I told you this was a no-fly zone."

Her hair was coming out of her ponytail, and her face was flushed. She was adorable.

"I'm here to help the homeless," he said innocently. He'd perfected that look with his grandma Helen.

Kenna scowled. "I have a fifteen-and-a-half-year-old son. Your innocent act doesn't hold water. I can't get out of this because Rosalie signs my checks. You have to bow out." Kenna plopped down on the pink couch, and the cat jumped on top of her. She started petting it even as she glared at Dex.

"Poppy, I'm not going to bow out. I'm going check out the homeless shelters with you next Saturday."

"Why would you do that? I told you I'm not interested."

"You wanted a snail's pace. This is it. We're not going on a date. We're going to churches and missions. I don't know how much more benign things could get. Or are you saying that's too risky for you? Are you afraid you'll throw yourself at me? Is that it?"

She pushed the cat off her lap and stood up.

"Why you arrogant...son of a sailor."

Dex laughed. "Grandson of a sailor, if you want to know the truth. And yes, I'll cop to the arrogant part. Are you going to throw yourself at me? If you are, shall we start now? This rug looks comfortable. I'm not sure I can handle making out on a pink sofa."

She opened her mouth. Then closed it. Then opened it again. "Fine, if you want to play this game, we'll play. But don't say I didn't warn you. My life is more complicated than a Rubik's cube. Rosalie is just one small part. I don't think you can keep up."

Bingo!

The beautiful woman in front of him had just issued a challenge. One he was dying to take up.

"My team's motto is 'the only easy day is yesterday.' I accept your challenge."

Her hazel eyes widened. "Wait a minute, isn't that the motto for the SEAL's?"

"Yep."

"You're a SEAL?"

Dex nodded.

"Crap! You're a player. I don't do players." He thought she might stomp her foot.

"What makes you think I'm a player?"

"I've heard stories. Two of the nurses at Sharp Memorial have dated SEALs. Total players."

Dex sighed. "I'm thirty-two. How old were they?"

"I don't know," she said as she bit her lip.

"Age makes a difference, don't you think? I told you, I'm not interested in a hook-up."

She planted her hands on her hips. Her womanly hips. Kenna had a hell of a figure. "You're in a dangerous profession."

"I also am away on missions I can't talk about. Those are the two negatives about my job. Other than that, I'm a homebody. I pick up after myself. I cook. I take out the garbage. I do the dishes. I pay my bills." Her eyes lit up on that last one. He'd said it on purpose. "Are you going to use my job as an excuse not to try this?"

"There is no *this*. And if there was, your job wouldn't be an issue. I would care about the man."

"And if I cared about a woman, her complicated life wouldn't be a problem for me. Let's get to know one another."

She kept her hands on her hips and scowled at him. "You're a pain in the ass."

The door opened, and Rosalie came in. She looked at Kenna's posture and smiled.

"I see you two are getting along. Kenna dear, the gardener has a question. I didn't understand everything he was saying. You understand some Spanish. If you could talk to him, that would be stupendous. Also, Ms. Ford from the Tribune wants to do a feature, can you call her back? I need to set up some time with Nancy for next week, be a dear and coordinate that would you?"

Kenna nodded.

"Aren't you going to write that down?" Dex asked.

Rosalie and Kenna both looked at him like he had lost his mind.

"Nonsense, Kenna always remembers everything." She turned back to Kenna. "Also, I want to discuss next Saturday's schedule. I think you need to start at the Union Mission and meet with Reverend Langley. You can give Dex your address so he can pick you up?"

"I'll drive myself."

"Nonsense. The mission is in Encanto. You shouldn't drive in that area alone. What's more, it will save on gas. Dex, I'll reimburse you for your time," she informed him imperiously.

"No, ma'am, you won't. This is my pleasure," he stated steadily.

Rosalie regarded him, taking his measure. Finally, she responded warmly. "I'm happy to hear that."

"You're nuts," Kenna mouthed at him.

Dex laughed.

CHAPTER FIVE

"Mom, what's the deal? Are you feeling okay?"

Kenna looked at her son in the reflection of her bathroom mirror. He was lounging against the doorjamb staring at her. His hair was tousled because he had just gotten out of bed.

"What makes you think I'm not feeling well?"

"I called your name like six times, and you didn't answer. And now I see you're putting on makeup to go to Rosalie's. Something's up."

Criminy. She was busted.

"It's just some mascara and lip gloss."

"You curled your hair."

She eyed herself in the mirror. She hadn't gone overboard, had she? Maybe she needed to put her hair in a ponytail like normal. She grabbed a scrunchie.

"Stop, you look nice."

She glanced up at Austin again.

"Ya think?"

"Denny would totally swallow his tongue if he saw you this morning. He already thinks you're hot."

Ewww. She didn't need to know that a fifteen-year-old boy thought she was hot. She grabbed her hair in one hand to put it up.

"Don't do that. Seriously, you look good with it down. Why are you changing things up?"

"I'm not going to Rosalie's. I'm meeting up with some people. Your grandmother will be here any minute."

"She's coming pretty early, isn't she?" Austin asked.

"I have to leave early. Somebody's going to pick me up."

The doorbell rang. They looked at one another.

"That must be your ride. Gram has a key," Austin stated the obvious.

Dammit. She'd texted Dex to wait at the curb, and she'd come out to him. She didn't want him to meet Austin. There were going to be too many questions.

She looked at her cell phone. Nope, no text from Dex, just another call from an unidentified caller. Couldn't Dex have texted to let her know he was coming to the door? This did not bode well if he couldn't follow one simple request.

Her son left to answer the door and she took another look in the mirror. Not too bad. Not as good as her profile pic, but not too bad. She swiped on another layer of lip gloss and hurried down the stairs.

Double damn. Her mother was at the bottom of the stairs beaming up at her. Dex was standing beside her, with a wide smile.

"Look who I found on your door step. You didn't tell me you were meeting a handsome man for breakfast." Penny Hartford said.

"I'm not," Kenna told her mother.

Dex let out a laugh. Austin and Penny joined him.

"Smooth Mom," Austin spoke at the same time her mother.

"Maybe you need your eyes checked, Kenna Leigh. He's handsome."

Kenna flushed. "We're not having breakfast," she mumbled.

"Dex, I'd like you to meet my son Austin, and my mother, Penny. Family, meet the handsome man, Dex Evans. We are *not* having breakfast. We are going to visit homeless shelters today. It's a new assignment for Rosalie."

"Actually, I was hoping we could pick up coffee and a scone. I told Reverend Langley we'd be there at nine," Dex smiled.

Austin gave her a sideways smirk. What was up with that? Shouldn't he be all upset that a strange man was trying to have coffee with her? She understood her mother's glee, but her son's?

"Dex, I thought I asked you to wait in the car for me this morning," she said pointedly.

"My grandfather would hand me my ass if I didn't go to a lady's door."

"You were raised right." Penny nodded firmly. "Did your grandfather raise you?"

"He had a large hand in it. I came out to San Diego most summers to spend them with my grandparents," Dex explained.

There was a story there.

"I can tell I like him," Penny said.

"Are you here to watch Austin while Kenna and I go do our thing?"

"Yep, that's my thing on Wednesdays and Saturdays. Let's me catch up with the light of my life. But today is a little more interesting."

"No. No, it isn't. It is just one of Rosalie's projects. Nothing interesting at all," Kenna said quickly.

The last thing she needed was her mother getting ideas.

"As a matter of fact, this is a big project that will take months. Rosalie has taken Kenna off all of her other duties to focus on this. I'll be spending pretty much all my free time coordinating with her. I'm really looking forward to it."

"In that case, you should come to dinner, shouldn't he Austin? I always cook on Saturdays since Kenna has to work."

Come on Baby Boy, do Mama a solid and say no.

Austin looked at her, then looked at Dex, then looked back at her. "Sounds good, Gram." He had a shit-eating grin on his face.

Traitor.

"Austin, I forgot to talk to you about some chores you need to get done today. Can you come with me?"

Kenna jerked her head towards the kitchen. He trailed her into the other room.

"What are you thinking?" she demanded. She had to stare up at him because he was three inches taller than her, but he was still her little boy.

"I'm thinking this is a way for Gram and me to see if he is make-up worthy."

"What?"

"You like him. It explains why you're wearing your hair down. I can cope. But this way I can see if he's a good guy. It's cool he didn't listen to you and came to the door. And Rosalie likes him. But then she likes everyone, so Gram and I need to vet him at dinner tonight."

She sank back against the counter and crossed her arms. "Are you sure you're only fifteen?"

"I'm going to be sixteen in two months. I've been the man of the family since forever."

"But. But. You were just worried about lucky socks," she protested she said as she spread her arms out.

"Mom. I'm a sophomore in high school. You give me the sex talk all the time. In two months, I'll have my driver's license. In a little over two years, I'll be in college. Hell, at that age you were pregnant with me."

Shit, she'd so been called out. "You're okay if this guy comes to dinner?"

"Do you like him?"

"He ticks me off."

"You like him." Austin grinned broadly. "We'll see you for dinner."

She stared up into hazel eyes that looked like a mirror of her own. "Look, don't grow up too fast, okay?"

"Don't worry, I haven't used the condoms."

Kenna's knees turned to water.

"Mom, I didn't mean it like that. I meant I haven't had sex yet. I meant I haven't grown up that much. Geez, I don't even have a steady girlfriend." Austin was twenty shades of red.

Kenna reached up and threw an arm around Austin's neck and kissed his temple. "Love you, Kid."

"Love you, Mom. See you for dinner. If you need condoms, you can have back the ones you gave me."

She turned twenty shades of red.

* * *

"You have a nice family," Dex said as he pulled into the Starbuck's parking lot.

"Thanks."

"What did your son say to you? You came out of the kitchen awfully flustered."

"He basically wants to check you out over dinner. Can you believe that?"

Dex opened the door for Kenna and put his hand on her lower back as they walked to the line. "Yes, I can believe that."

Her head swiveled up to look at him. "You can?"

"Yep. Any man would want to make sure they approved of the guy that their daughter, sister or mother was going out with. It's in our DNA."

"He's not a man. He's a boy."

They placed their orders.

"Can I pay?" Dex asked when Kenna reached for her wallet. She bit her lip but then acquiesced. "Thank you," he said.

They waited for their drinks and scones.

"Austin struck me as a level-headed young man who got along with both you and your mother, but he's also awfully protective of you."

"You got all of that from just fifteen minutes?" Kenna's pretty eyes looked at him curiously.

"Yep. What did he say to you in the kitchen?"

"He wants me to have a social life, and he liked that you came to the door."

The kid was perceptive. "When was the last time you went on a date?"

Kenna's gaze slid away from his. She looked over at the barista.

"Kenna?"

"It's been awhile."

"How long?"

"A date that was make-up worthy? Too damn long. I told you this was not a good idea. You met Rosalie, you met Austin. My life is complicated with a capital 'C.' Then I work four tens on Monday, Tuesday, Thursday, and Friday."

"So? You have a life." Dex shrugged. He was not going to be put off no matter how many obstacles she threw in his path.

"Let's not forget my neurosis."

"Why haven't you been on a make-up worthy date if you're signed up on CaliSingles? That doesn't make sense."

"Dex!" the barista attendant yelled out. Dex snagged their beverages and pastries. When he got back to Kenna, he could see that she was regretting what she had shared. A wall had gone down.

Damn.

"Wanna eat on the way to the mission?" he asked.

She gave a relieved nod. Even so, she didn't balk when he put his hand on her lower back and guided her to his jeep and opened the door for her and helped her inside. She was flustered. Flustered was good, it was better than having a wall.

He drove to Encanto. Even during the early morning hours, it was a less than welcoming area. He was glad that she was not driving in her own car.

"This place looks like it could use the two million plus another ten," Kenna said when they pulled up to the brick building. It was surrounded by a rusted chain link fence with plenty of holes in it.

She was not wrong.

"How many people did Reverend Langley say they served in a year?"

Kenna pulled out her smart phone. "Over twelve thousand. That's crazy. It's so small."

"Let's go inside." He liked the fact that she allowed him to guide her into the building. He was fast becoming addicted to touching her. She fit him. She came up to his shoulder. Her hair looked good down around her shoulders. Kenna had been wrong, she looked even better than her picture on the dating site.

As soon as they opened the doors to the building, Dex could hear the yelling. There was a problem.

"Get back in the jeep, and lock the doors."

"What is it?" Kenna asked.

"Just do what I say," he commanded.

She gave him a questioning look as he shoved the keys at her.

"Do I need to call nine-one-one?"

"Yes."

She grabbed the keys and headed back to the jeep. Dex carefully pushed open the interior double doors. Three men were beating a fourth man, it was brutal. He saw Reverend Langley holding back a woman who was trying to wade in. He shoved the doors open and rushed in.

"Do something. Somebody help!" she screamed.

There were at least thirty people standing around, nobody was doing anything.

Reverend Langley was in his mid-sixties. If he tried to stop them, he would be pummeled.

Dex didn't hesitate.

The man they were beating was as big as Hunter, but he was being held by two men, while the third was using him as a punching bag. As the guy brought back his fist to deliver another blow, Dex grabbed his arm, twisted him around and delivered a hit to his face. He fell to the floor like a sack of wet cement. Dex felt someone coming up behind him, and he looked over his shoulder as he jammed his elbow into the man's gut. The man grunted but reached for Dex anyway.

In a flash, Dex had the man flipped onto his back, and staring at the ceiling. He heard sirens as he turned toward the third man, and saw who fighting with the victim. Any other day of the year, the huge Hispanic man would have wiped the floor with the scruffy blond guy, but he was seriously injured. He waded in, grabbing the blonde by the neck and flung him into the wall.

"Watch out!" It was Kenna's voice. She was close. Too damned close.

Something metal hit Dex on his side. A chair. He saw a fourth guy holding a metal chair over his head. Easy enough to deflect, except for the fact that he saw Kenna was reaching for the fucking thing.

"Kenna, get back!"

The man turned and swung the chair as he went. Dex barely pulled it out of his arms in time to stop him from hitting her. As it was, he lost his balance and fell into her, and took her to the floor. Dex pulled him off Kenna by his arm and hair.

"Oww!" the man cried. Dex hit him in the mouth, shutting him up.

"Police! Everybody freeze!"

Dex dropped the man and knelt beside Kenna who was lifting herself up on her elbows.

"Are you all right?" She shook her head. He couldn't tell if it was an answer, or she was trying to clear her head.

In the background, he heard Reverend Langley talking to the cops, but all his attention was focused on Kenna. He cupped her head gently in his hands and touched the back of her scalp with his fingertips. She winced. She'd gone down hard.

She struggled to get up.

"Stay down."

"No, I need to get up."

"No, you need to stay where you are until the EMTs can come and check you out. You hit your head pretty hard, and probably have a concussion."

She gave him an incredulous look. "Are you out of your mind?"

That's when it hit him. "Are you out of yours?" he asked fiercely. "I told you to stay in the jeep. What were you doing coming back in here? You could have been killed."

She pushed at his hands. "Again. I reiterate. Are you out of your mind? There were no weapons. It was just a fight."

He looked at the small woman who was struggling against him to get up. His mind went back to that moment when the man was aiming the chair at her.

"That chair could have hit you in the head and killed you!" he roared. "When I tell you to stay in the jeep, you stay in the fucking jeep."

"Cool your jets big guy," Kenna said as she once again tried to sit up. "I'm the mother of a teenage boy, I know how to take care of myself and break up a fight."

A police officer crouched down beside them. "Is she all right?"

"I'm fine."

"She needs to be checked out by an EMT," Dex answered.

"We have medics on the way. They should be coming any second," the cop answered.

"You're making too big of a deal of this," Kenna huffed.

The officer looked at Dex. "What happened?"

Dex gave him a quick version of the events.

"Ma'am, you should have stayed in the car," the officer said to Kenna after Dex was done with his explanation.

"Look, I don't need all of you males ganging up on me," Kenna growled.

"Over here," the cop motioned when the medics arrived.

Kenna looked over Dex's shoulder and moaned.

"Are you in pain?" he asked.

"Yes. I don't see a female medic. I'm surrounded by testosterone. I swear Dex if one more man gives me shit, I'm going to scream."

The police officer coughed. Dex knew he was covering up a laugh.

"It's okay, Poppy. No one else will give you a hard time. We just want to make sure you're okay."

He wasn't as concerned as he had been initially. She didn't look pale, disoriented, just frustrated. Dex really thought that the EMTs were going to give her a clean bill of health, but still, he wanted her checked out.

"What?" Kenna asked him.

"What do you mean, 'what'?" Dex asked.

"You're looking at me funny."

"Just looking at your pretty face."

She snorted and turned to the young man who knelt beside her. "Don't forget to check out Dex. He took some hits during the fight. I think he might have suffered some brain trauma."

The cop covered another laugh.

* * *

Kenna found herself drinking coffee for the second time that morning thanks to Reverend Langley providing some in his office after the police and EMTs had cleared out.

"I am so sorry that you arrived when we had violence going on."

The clergyman looked awfully tired, and Kenna felt bad for him.

"Does this type of thing happen often?" Dex asked.

"We used to have a good security team that worked around the clock. We had to cut back. Now they work at night. In the morning we count on volunteers, but unfortunately, our two volunteers didn't show up this morning."

Kenna held the Styrofoam cup of coffee in both hands so that neither man would see her hands tremble. She still wasn't one hundred percent since the fight, but she didn't need their focus. Luckily, her voice was steady as she asked, "what other cuts have you had to make?"

"We have beds and mattresses, but as we move into the winter, we won't be able to turn up the heat like we need to. We're constantly making choices between food and utilities. It's a balancing act. I know you're going to go to some of the other shelters today. They need some funds as well, but in Encanto, we have to depend on government resources because our community is poor. The government resources have been drying up over the last three years. I hope that you will see your way clear to help us."

Dex leaned forward, elbows on his knees, and listened to every word the Reverend said. As he ended his speech, he looked sideways at Kenna. "What are you thinking?" he asked her.

"Do you have a budget showing what your funding was three years ago, and where you stand today?" she asked.

The reverend went to a computer on his desk. He gave a sheepish grin. "Despite my complaints, I have made sure we are connected to the internet. I'll e-mail you what you requested if you provide me your address."

"Reverend, having internet access is a necessity," Kenna assured him. She set her coffee down on the floor beside her purse and took out a business card. Then she stood to walk it over to his desk and wobbled just the slightest bit.

Before she had a chance to right herself, Dex had his arm around her waist. It helped. It ticked her off, but the helping part took precedence. He took the card out of her hand and held it out to Reverend Langley.

"I'm so sorry you both were hurt at my mission," he said with a frown.

"It's nothing," she assured him.

"I'm taking her home after this. We'll visit the other facilities next Saturday. Kenna has had enough excitement for one day."

The sad part was, Dex was probably right. But she didn't want to go home and worry her family. Maybe Rosalie's house?

They were soon out in the San Diego sunlight without her sunglasses, it hurt her eyes.

"Let's get you home," Dex said. He still had his warm arm surrounding her, and she took advantage of it. It felt good to lean on someone for a change.

"If I'm not checking out the other shelters, I should really work. Take me to Rosalie's," she requested, looking at him as they stood in front of his jeep.

He looked at her and gave her a considering look.

"Rosalie would definitely not want you working today. She'd want you to take it easy."

"I can take it easy at Rosalie's house," she said firmly.

His brown eyes assessed her. She saw the minute he saw through her.

"You don't want to go home and worry Austin and your mom, am I right?"

"No, I don't. Take me to Rosalie's. She'll arrange for a ride back to my home tonight."

"If I take you to Rosalie's, will you rest?"

"Yes," she lied firmly.

"Bullshit. It's a madhouse over at Rosalie's. You're coming home with me, where I can make sure you take a nap."

"It is not a madhouse."

"Are you telling me that Smooches won't try to climb all over you, and you won't have to translate for the gardener?"

"It's either my house or your house, which is it?" he asked.

She sighed and shook her head. Even that small motion hurt. "Hell Dex, you don't even know me, and you're treating this like it was a Las Vegas fight. If I go home and say, I'm woozy because I got knocked down by some bruiser down in Encanto, Austin will lose his mind." She blew out a breath.

"I knew I liked that kid."

Kenna tried to twist out of Dex's hold, but it didn't work. He didn't hold onto her roughly, just firmly. Firmly and gently. How did he manage that?

Kenna bent her head so she wouldn't have to look in his eyes, but he was having none of it. He put his knuckle under her chin and tipped it up.

"Look at me, Poppy."

"That's a stupid nickname," she complained because she liked the feel of his hand on her face.

"Look at me."

"No."

"What? Are you five?"

"Poppy makes me sound like a five-year-old."

"It makes you sound like a firecracker, all pop, fizz, and fire."

Her eyes shot up to look at him.

"Are you for real?"

"Lady, you've been tangling me up since the first damned e-mail with all of your attitude. I was worried that you wouldn't be as good in person, but you're even better."

He was the one who was better in person. She'd damned near swallowed her tongue when she'd seen him in jeans and the Henley this morning. Then to see him wade in on that fight, so sure and so in command. Holy hell!

She shook her head to clear it. Pain shot through her brain.

"Can we stop off at the pharmacy and get some ibuprofen? I don't have any in my purse, and the medic said it would help with a headache."

"My place is ten minutes from here. I have ibuprofen, and it's only twenty minutes from here, so that's where we're going. We're done discussing this," Dex said as he opened the door to his jeep. He helped her in.

* * *

"Honey, we're here."

Kenna opened her eyes and saw flowers, lots and lots of deep pink and purple buds.

"Where are we?" She asked the question of Dex not taking her eyes off the mounds of bougainvillea flowers surrounding the carport.

"We're at my townhome. My grandmother has a green thumb. She said that this would look nice. I'm lucky that I can still park my bike under the carport." Kenna peered in and saw that there was, indeed, a motorcycle parked there.

"This is amazing."

"Let's get you inside. I want you to have your medicine and a nap. You fell asleep two seconds after I started the jeep."

"I'm fine now. I'm awake," she protested. She might have won the argument if she hadn't yawned. He just raised his eyebrows and slowly shook his head. Kenna was still struggling with her seatbelt when Dex came around the other side of the jeep and opened the door.

"Do you need help?"

"No, I don't need help," she said belligerently. Luckily the hook came unlatched, and she pushed it off. He held out his hand, but she shoved it aside and got out of the vehicle on her own.

"Slow down, Poppy."

"Quit calling me that." God, she *did* sound like a cranky five-year-old.

"If you quit popping off, I'd quit calling you Poppy."

She glared at his grin. He pointed toward the carport, and she saw the side door. He let her in, and once again, her breath was taken away. Not by flowers this time, but by the indoor jungle.

"It seems that you have a green thumb too."

"Not really. My cousin's daughter, Andrea, takes care of my plants when I'm gone, and they multiply like rabbits, then she brings in more. I'm afraid one day I'll come back from a mission, and I'll have nowhere to sleep."

She watched as he got a glass from the kitchen cupboard, and then reach into another cupboard and pull out a bottle of pills. "Let's get you your meds, and then you can lie down in the guest room."

"I don't want to put you out," she protested.

Weak!

Now that she was here, she totally wanted to check out his home. What did that make her? *Weak!* She watched as he filled the glass with water from the fridge, then handed her the glass and pills.

"Drink up."

She did.

"Seriously, how are you feeling? And don't feed me a line of shit."

Kenna grimaced, and Dex grinned. "How'd you know I was going to lie?" she asked.

"Everybody always says they're 'fine.' It's the first response no matter what. You were opening your mouth before your brain was engaged. So now that you're thinking about it, how are you feeling? You were a little unsteady in Reverend Langley's office."

"I'm not used to being tackled on a linoleum floor. Austin and I used to play pig pile, but it was always on a rug. So yeah, just a short nap, and I'll be good."

His brown eyes warmed at her answer. "I imagine that wrestling on the floor with Austin was a long time ago, judging by the size of him."

"It seems like just yesterday, and forever ago."

He nodded like he understood. "Come on, let's get you your nap."

He led her down a short hall to a nicely furnished guest room. "The bathroom is right here," he said opening the door directly across from the room. "Now that I earned a free morning, I've got a couple of things that need my attention. I'll be communing with my computer in my study when you wake up. It's the room right off the living room." He gave her hand a squeeze. "If you can't find me, just holler."

She watched as he shut the door behind him, and she sank down on the bed.

Dexter Anthony Evans. Thirty-two. Never been married. Lived in San Diego his entire life. Buddy had said he could probably get a copy of his medical file if she wanted. But she didn't need that to know he was in phenomenal shape. If it weren't for the fact that she had caught him looking at her twice like he wanted to eat her up with a spoon, she would slink away in mortification at the idea of them together. He was physical perfection.

Buddy had also confirmed that what he had stated on the dating profile were true. He volunteered at the Big Brothers

Big Sisters of San Diego, the boy he had been mentoring was currently a sophomore at Cal State Fullerton, and Dex wasn't rushing into starting a new relationship.

Dex had graduated from UNLV, with a double major in computer engineering and mathematics, but instead of going the Navy ROTC officer route, he graduated and the next day joined the Navy as an enlisted man. According to everything that Buddy ascertained, he wanted to end his career the same as his grandfather, a master chief petty officer.

Every damn thing that Buddy had found out about Mr. Evans screamed honor. Kenna wasn't worried about her physical well-being while staying at his house for a nap, but she was worried about her mental well-being.

She was interested in the damned man. What in the hell was she thinking?! She shook her head in disgust and winced.

"Lie down and quit obsessing," she admonished herself.

She toed off her Sketchers and slid under the duvet. It felt like heaven. Damn, she was more tired than she'd realized. Double damn, he even had comfy linens.

* * *

He'd missed a Skype call from Darryl. Dex tried to ring him back but was stuck leaving a message. After that, he settled into the project he'd been working on for the mentoring program. It was a real bitch of a project, and he was enjoying the hell out of it. First, the old system that they had used to keep track of their applicants in San Diego was developed twenty years ago. They'd just done facelifts to it, instead of revamping it.

One of his buddies from college had gotten a job at a start-up in San Francisco and had contributed state of the art hardware, and he'd tapped another friend to cough up some sweet software to go on top of it. Now it was up to Dex to migrate everything. There had been some unplanned hiccups that had pissed him off. Who would have thought that they would not have deleted access to their system to severed employees over the last four years? The second thing was when he found out that their backups had been going to discs that were out of storage space, and instead of being over-ridden, the backups just weren't getting done. They'd been walking a tight-rope without a net for over eight months.

He was monitoring the systems while thinking about Kenna. Seeing her in person had been a revelation. Here she had been talking about how she couldn't replicate her 'look' when all along she rang his bell wearing no make-up with her hazel eyes spitting fire and attitude. Okay, if he had to put a fine point on the matter, today with her hair down he was a happier man. But still, she was a knock-out. And she had no idea. She walked into the Starbucks with him and had no earthly idea that she was garnering a ton of male attention. How in the hell was that possible? If he had to guess it had something to do with that asshat of an ex-husband.

He was midway through a line of code when he heard the door to the guest room open. He looked at the computer clock and saw that it was a little after noon. Dex hoped that Kenna was hungry because he was starved.

"Can I take you to lunch?" Kenna asked as she walked into his office.

"I was about to ask you the same thing. But I'm ecstatic to have you ask me out on a date." He grinned.

Dex watched as she blushed and scowled at the same time. The scowl won out. "You know I was just offering to pay for lunch to return your hospitality."

"Are you sure? Maybe subconsciously you wanted to ask me out all along."

Her eyes got wide. "My God, you're full of yourself, aren't you?"

He laughed. "You're fun to tease."

"Well stop it," she grumbled. "Do you want lunch or not?"

"Yep. Do you like Mexican food?" He ushered her back towards the living room. "I have to insist on buying your lunch since you're feeding me dinner."

"Dutch treat. That way we're not indebted to one another."

"How's your head feeling?" he asked changing the subject.

"It was feeling fine until you started teasing me. Seriously, we're not dating. We're just having lunch."

"Go get your shoes and purse, and we'll argue our status over lunch. Or should we argue about it after dinner? Two meals in one day seems kind of significant."

"You're right it does. Hold on while I call my mother and tell her you can't make it for dinner," she shot over her shoulder as she headed back to the guest room.

Dex grinned. He was ninety-nine percent sure she was giving him shit, but the fact that he wasn't totally sure made it all the more entertaining.

"If I agree to split the lunch bill, am I still invited to dinner?" he asked Kenna when she came back the hall.

"It depends on how well you behave at lunch. If you give me too hard of a time, then dinner is off."

He opened the door for her, and they went out to the jeep. He watched as she admired the bougainvillea again. "I can take you to a chain restaurant, or this little dive that has great food. Your choice."

"Definitely the dive," Kenna answered. "Austin and I eat at this one taco truck at least twice a month. It has the best food."

"I wasn't sure since you said that you worked hard to live in a good neighborhood." Dex backed out onto the street and headed toward Danny's Taqueria.

"Four years ago, at our old house, Austin was playing with the kids in our neighborhood. They were a grade older than he was. I was good with it because he was going to be in middle school with them, but it turned out two of them were in a gang. One of the boys shot a convenience store clerk. We were renting a small house, I moved out the next week."

"You didn't have an idea of where you were going to move to?"

"I must have talked to everyone at the nursing home and school I was going to, pretty soon I figured out the right middle school and high school for Austin to attend. All I could afford was an apartment, but I moved us in."

"You didn't let any grass grow under your feet."

"Absolutely not. Austin hated leaving his friends and living in an apartment, but he knew I was trying to do the right thing for us, so he sucked it up."

Dex maneuvered over the potholes in the cramped parking lot. "I'll say it again, Austin seems like a good kid."

"I think he is, but I'm biased."

She moved a little more slowly than usual out of the jeep, and he opened the door to the small restaurant. "We place our orders up front," he explained.

"It smells great in here." Her hazel eyes lit up. "Is there anything you recommend?"

"Some kind of seafood. Their fish tacos are fantastic. I'm getting the shrimp rancheros. I'm also ordering guacamole with some of their homemade flour tortillas. Chips are free, but I slather the guac on my tortillas."

"You talked me into the fish tacos."

"Good choice." They placed their orders, and Kenna didn't even complain when he pulled out his wallet and paid for the meal. When he took their number, and they sat down at a table, he couldn't resist.

"Now that we're on our first date tell me more about yourself."

She placed her elbow on the table and planted her chin in her hand. "I would love to after you tell me why you decided to contact me on the dating site. What about my profile stood out to you?"

Fuck! How in the hell was he going to answer that one?

"Dex? It's an easy enough question. I looked at your profile, it had only been up for one day before you contacted me. Why me?"

Holy hell, he didn't want to start this off on some kind of lie, but he didn't want to have her think that he didn't think she was special.

He was relieved when their number was called for their drinks. By the time he sat down Kenna was pissed.

"What?"

She looked him up and down, her face was flushed. Her hands were now clenched on the table in front of her. "Consider your words carefully Dexter Evans, I don't deal well with liars."

"Does Austin get away with anything with you?"

"Not that I know of," she bit out.

She unrolled her napkin and slammed the plastic utensils down on the table. "I thought it was weird that someone like you would reach out to someone like me right after joining the site. But you were so funny and nice I overlooked it. But now you can't answer one damned question without hesitating. What gives?"

Dex reached over and grabbed her right hand, and pulled it to him. He waited until she unclenched it and he was able to sandwich it between both of his.

"Kenna, at this moment, I am right where I want to be. I want to go out with you. Everything I've said to you after you sent me your e-mail has been the absolute truth. Does that pass the smell test?"

"So, you didn't send the initial e-mail?"

Dex's laugh made people turn their heads to look at him. "God, nobody can accuse you of being slow. You caught that, did you?"

"I have a teenage son, I'm trained to read through bullshit. Who sent me the first e-mail?"

"Guys from another SEAL team were playing a joke and set up the account, they sent hundreds of e-mails to women on that site. Over two hundred women responded, and I spent three nights explaining that it was a fake account and that I really hadn't pinged their profile."

Dex was hopeful when Kenna didn't try to pull her hand away.

"That was a hell of a prank. You actually responded back to those women? How did that go?" Her eyes were twinkling.

"Mostly okay."

"I'm thinking there might be a story with the ones that didn't go 'okay.'"

Dex shrugged. "I learned a couple of new phrases, and considering the fact that I'm in the Navy, that's saying something."

Kenna giggled. Then she got serious. "Why didn't you blow me off?"

"You made me laugh. I'd never considered a dating site, but if I'd known you were on one, I would have been there years ago." He looked down at their clasped hands, then back into her eyes.

"Kenna, all I was doing was reading e-mails and responding. Then I read yours and thought this is someone I have to meet. Of course, I had to go look at your profile pic since you swore it was the bomb..."

"I did not." She tried to pull her hand away, but he wouldn't let her.

"I wanted to see what twenty dollars' worth of product looked like. It was pretty damn spectacular."

"So, it was the picture." She smiled at him.

"It was the triple threat. A good mother, a killer smile, and someone who could make me laugh. I had to meet you. Then you took down your profile."

She tugged at her hand again. Their number was called, so he let her go and went to the counter. When he came back with the food, she was looking thoughtful.

"Before you say whatever it is you're going to say. Eat." He pushed her plate of food in front of her. "It's better when it's hot."

"But I'm not all—"

"You're all that and a bag of chips."

"A bag of chips." She laughed. She had a great laugh. "Seriously Dex, you listen—"

"Nope, don't want to hear it. I'm not going to like it, I can tell. I want to enjoy my lunch. You can ruin my digestion after the fact. I have Rolaids in my jeep."

"Seriously, Dex."

"Seriously, Kenna," he mimicked her. "You're going to say something stupid about not giving this a shot for some inane reason, and I won't be hungry. Right now, I'm hungry, and I'm about to eat one of my favorite meals, don't ruin it for me, I'm begging you."

She unwrapped her straw and put it into her drink. "All right. It does smell good," she admitted.

He smiled. Now to get her talking about something else, and they would have their first date!

CHAPTER SIX

"Rosalie, I'm driving. It's rainy. I'm going to be late for work. I don't have time for this."

"You've been avoiding my calls for days. I'm not going to see you until tomorrow. Tell me how Saturday went. You told me you're physically fine. But I want to know how it went with the dashing Navy man."

"Traffic is horrible this morning. I'll talk to you tomorrow when I'm at your house."

"Don't you dare hang up on me. He came over to your house for dinner. How did it go with Austin?"

"Austin wants to be a SEAL now. Okay? I'll talk to you tomorrow."

"You better."

Kenna pressed the button on her steering wheel that ended the call. She should have never answered in the first place, not with the rain coming down like it was. God knew that they needed the rain here in Southern California, but having to drive on the freeways during rush hour was not fun. Her cell phone rang again when she was parking her car.

What the hell?

She grabbed her phone to answer it and give Rosalie a piece of her mind.

"Rosalie, I'll talk to you tomorrow."

"This isn't Rosalie," a man answered.

Kenna dropped the keys to her car as she was getting out. She said eighty million swear words as they hit the water-logged parking lot.

"Who is this?" Kenna asked as she picked up her keys and pulled out her umbrella.

"A friend of a friend." The man's voice was low and raspy.

What a strange answer. She looked down and realized she had answered a call that was unidentified. "Seriously, who is this? What's this about?"

She didn't hear his whole answer as she fumbled with her purse, keys, and umbrella.

"...for a long time," were the words he said as she put the phone back up to her ear.

"Can you repeat that?"

"Are you ignoring me?" he asked in that same quiet, creepy tone.

"I just didn't hear you."

She was then met by silence.

She looked down, the call had ended.

Huh? Dumbass probably thought he was talking to some-one else.

She got to the hospital and was making her way to the ele-vator when Patsy Harns rushed up to her.

"Did you hear?" Patsy's eyes were bright with tears.

"Hear what?" Kenna asked as she shook out her raincoat.

"Jean's dead. She was murdered."

Kenna dropped her coat on the floor. "What?"

"There are cops here, they're asking people questions."

Kenna bent and slowly picked up her coat, hugging it close. "Murdered?" she whispered. "Somebody killed her?"

"It happened over the weekend. When she didn't show up to her appointments on Monday, they sent Abby to check on her when she didn't answer her phone. She has a key to her house. It was bad."

"What do you mean bad?" Kenna asked.

Patsy started to cry. "Abby said she was tortured. Doctor Larkin took her home and gave her a sedative."

Kenna couldn't comprehend what Patsy was saying. It made no sense. Jean Baldwin was her friend. She just finished her residency last year. She was thinking about moving to Philadelphia to be close to her dad. She was not dead.

"Patsy, are you sure?"

The elevator opened and the charge nurse for the on-cology floor came out, along with two men Kenna didn't rec-ognize.

"Kenna, do you have a moment? I saw you walking in from the parking lot. I wanted to catch you before you came up to the floor. These two police detectives want to talk to you."

Kenna looked at her boss and then at the two cops. "Okay," she said slowly.

Please, let this be a bad dream.

"Why don't you take them to the cafeteria," the woman suggested gently.

"This is about Jean, isn't it?" Kenna said staring at them.

"Ms. Wright, let's discuss this over a cup of coffee, all right?" The smaller of the two men smiled at her.

Kenna nodded. She pointed toward the hallway. Her hand was trembling. "The cafeteria is down there."

"We know this is difficult. Please take a seat." They allowed her to take a few moments to settle before they introduced themselves. Detectives Warren and Sanchez were working the murder of Dr. Jean Baldwin.

Detective Warren went and got them coffee, and when he returned Kenna looked at the two men and asked the question that was on her mind.

"But I don't understand, are you having coffee with all of the nurses who worked with Jean?" Kenna asked.

"We wanted to ask you about an e-mail that she forwarded to you. It was from a dating site."

"Do you think I might be of help in solving her murder?" she asked.

"Right now, we're investigating everything. Any information, any insights, that you can provide would be greatly appreciated."

Kenna stirred her coffee and thought about the e-mail. Then she looked at the detectives. "Why are you asking me about it, you've read it, haven't you?"

"What Clive meant was, what did Jean have to say about the guy? She must have said something. Otherwise, she wouldn't have forwarded the e-mail to you," Detective Sanchez clarified.

"She wanted my take on him. I said surface-wise he seemed okay. I looked at his profile. But his e-mail seemed like he was trying too hard for somebody who was supposedly an attorney. I told her to use caution. Will this help you in finding out who killed her? Do you think it could have been him?" Kenna took a sip of her coffee and tried hard not to wiggle in her seat as the two men examined her.

"How were you able to look at his profile? You don't have a profile on CaliSingles."

"I did at the time she sent me the e-mail. I've taken it down since then. You didn't answer my question."

"We really can't answer your questions. This is an ongoing investigation, and we're just following up on any and all leads."

Made sense.

Kenna nodded.

"If you told her to proceed with caution, would it surprise you to learn that she continued to correspond with him?"

"No," she answered.

She watched as Detective Warren made notes. "Why didn't it surprise you?" he asked.

"What I meant when I said to proceed with caution was that she needed to do a lot of questioning. Hopefully, if you read through her e-mails, you'll see where she was trying to see if he was for real or not."

"Did she ever talk to you about him again?"

Kenna thought back and finally answered, "no."

"How about other men from the dating site?"

"No."

"Other men in general?"

"The last time we talked was about this attorney." Then it hit her. That was the last time that she was ever going to talk to Jean. She pushed away her coffee and covered her mouth.

Oh God.

Jean was dead.

"Ms. Wright, are you okay?" Detective Warren asked.

She nodded. Then she shook her head. "No," Kenna answered. She closed her eyes and tried breathing through her mouth until she could focus, then she opened her eyes and looked at the men sitting across from her.

They were patient as they waited for her to get control. She grabbed a napkin out of the dispenser and blew her nose.

"Is there anything else you can tell us about Jean. Not just the e-mail, but any men she has seen recently?" Detective Sanchez asked. "Where else does she meet men?"

Kenna thought about it. "She didn't want to date guys here at the hospital, so she joined Fresh Fitness gym. She's been going for the last four months. She told me about two guys from there."

The detective made notes as she told him everything she could remember about the two men.

"Any bars or clubs? How about volunteer agencies?" Detective Warren asked.

"The only other thing besides the dating site and the gym she mentioned was that she was going to go sailing. But I didn't follow up on that. She was single, but she didn't want to be. Ever since she finished her residency, she wanted to find a man to settle down with. If I'd been a better friend, I would have kept up with her better."

She was dead. Kenna couldn't stop thinking about that.

Jean was dead.

"We've been interviewing the people in her life, you sound like a good friend to her, Ms. Wright," Detective Sanchez said.

Detective Warren pulled out a card and slid it across the table to her. "If you think of anything else, please give us a call."

Kenna nodded.

* * *

When she took a break, she found five messages on her cell phone. Three from her mother and two from Rosalie. They all concerned Jean. Apparently, it had made the news that a doctor from Sharp Memorial had been murdered.

She called her mother first.

"Kenna, are you all right?"

"I'm fine."

"This was your friend Jean, wasn't it? The one who came to our house two years ago for Halloween?"

Kenna swallowed. She remembered how Jean had wanted to hand out candy. She'd met Austin. "Yes Mom, that's her."

"I'm so sorry. When are the services?"

"I'll let you know." She thought her dad would want them in Philadelphia, but she couldn't think about it right now.

"Are you doing all right, Honey?"

Kenna settled at the sound of her mother's tone.

"Yeah."

"Have someone walk you out to your car tonight."

"Mom, it'll still be daylight when I get off work," she protested.

"Just do that for me."

Kenna pressed a thumb against her temple. "I will."

"I'll see you tomorrow night when I watch Austin."

"See you tomorrow, Mom. I love you."

"Love you too, Honey."

She hung up and called Rosalie and got her voicemail. She left a message and went back to work. When she finished her shift for the day, Patsy sidled up to her.

"Let's walk out together," she suggested.

"Did you get a lecture too?" Kenna asked with a laugh.

"What are you talking about?" Patsy asked, clearly confused. "I'll just feel better if I have someone to walk with me to the parking lot."

Kenna ducked her head. "Oh. Yeah, that makes sense," she agreed.

She walked with Patsy to her Prius and the woman then insisted on driving Kenna to her car. It was clear she was really freaked.

"You know that this didn't happen here. It happened at her house," Kenna tried to reassure the woman.

"We don't know that he didn't target her from the hospital," Patsy said.

It was true. But still, it all seemed like overkill to Kenna. All that mattered was that Jean was dead. She sucked in air through her nose, trying to keep it together.

She got out of Patsy's car and leaned in. "Thanks. I'll see you on Thursday."

"Not tomorrow?" Patsy asked.

"I work four tens. I'm off on Wednesdays," Kenna reminded her.

"Oh yeah. You work longer hours than me, so I guess carpooling is out."

"It's going to be okay, Patsy. They'll get this guy."

"I know. I'm just antsy."

"Well, when I am here at the hospital, I will definitely walk with you to and from your car. You have my number, right?"

Patsy nodded.

"Good. Thanks for the lift." Kenna shut the door and waved.

She got into her car and immediately locked the car doors, then took a deep breath.

She bent her head and said a soft prayer for her dead friend, then started her car.

* * *

Getting Austin to bed that night had taken longer than normal. They'd talked for a while. Initially, Kenna thought it was because Jean had made an impression on him, and he needed to process the fact that she was now dead, but she soon realized that wasn't it. He needed reassurance that she was safe. Hopefully, she'd been able to provide that to him.

She waited until he was asleep before tears fell. It wasn't fair. It just wasn't fair. Jean was a beautiful person, inside and out, and she should be alive.

Kenna wandered through the house, swiping at her face, turning off all the lights and heading for bed. She was under the covers when she went to set the alarm on her phone, that was when she noticed she'd missed a call from Dex. She debated calling him back so late. Didn't SEAL's have to be up early?

Then she saw the text.

Poppy,

I'm worried, was the doctor at the hospital a friend of yours? Do you need to talk?

She replied.

Yes, Jean is a friend of mine. I'm fine.

Dammit, she'd talked in the present tense. Jean's dead, she reminded herself.

Her phone vibrated. It was Dex.

"Are you okay?" His voice was warm and worried.

"Yeah." She settled against the pillows of her bed.

"Ahhh Honey, I'm so sorry for your friend." He paused, his voice went lower. "For you."

"All I keep thinking about is her poor dad and being thankful that her mom is dead. It would kill her. Here I am happy that Jean's mom is dead. What kind of monster does that make me?"

"Human. It makes you human and compassionate."

"Thank you," she let out a breath. There was a long silence. "I'm glad you texted me. I wasn't going to call you back. I thought you'd be asleep."

"Why didn't you think I would be awake?" he asked. He had changed to a teasing tone. She needed it. She sank deeper into her pillows.

"Usually we talk about eight o'clock. Don't you have to hit the base early?"

"Yeah, but I operate on about six hours of sleep a night."

Now she was thinking about his sleeping habits. Not a good thing. Time to change the direction of this conversation.

"Austin and mom want you to come over to dinner again this Saturday."

"I'd like a little alone time with you. I'll do a meal with the fam on Sunday if I can have a date with you on Saturday."

"We're going to see each other from eight to two on Saturday when we visit the facilities, isn't that too much time?"

"No." Immediate. Decisive.

"What happened to a snail in peanut butter?" she asked.

"Isn't that what the French eat?" She could hear the smile in his voice.

She liked it. She'd been liking all of their calls.

"I don't think the French eat escargot in peanut butter, Dex."

"We're going slow. We're still in the getting to know you stage. Last Saturday we had a lunch date, and I got to have a meal with you, your mom and your son. This week, we'll have a dinner date and a meal with your son and mom over at my place. I'll grill. Let's have Rosalie too, so it doesn't feel too intimate. I promised a couple of the guys some meat at my place. It'll just be a backyard barbeque. No family I promise."

She pushed up on her pillows.

"Family?" she squeaked.

"I was going to suggest you come over to my grandparents on Sunday for the family barbeque, but I figured that would freak you out."

"Well yes, meeting your family would definitely freak me out," she said weakly.

"Come on over to my place, and I'll grill."

"Could we skip the date, and just do the grilling?"

"No way. I thought every woman likes to play dress-up."

"It's a dress up kind of date?" Her voice went up an octave.

"If your voice goes any higher, I'll think you're auditioning to be a soprano. Yep, it'll be fancy. How does that sound?"

It sounded good.

It sounded bad.

It sounded scary.

"Kenna?"

"What?"

"Will you go out with me on Saturday?"

She blew out a breath. "This isn't slow," she admonished. "How about another lunch date," she suggested hopefully.

"You're braver than that, Kenna."

Damn, he had a great voice.

"Come on Kenna. It's a date for dinner. I dare you."

She sank back into her pillows. "Are you always going to dare me SailorBoy?"

"Yes Poppy, if it will get me what I want."

"What time are you going to pick me up?"

"Six."

She didn't have a nice dress. She had presentable. She had PTA. She didn't have Navy nice.

"Kenna, you with me?"

"I'm here."

"You won't bail, will you?"

"You dared me, didn't you?"

"I would have double dog dared you if necessary. But I was holding that in reserve."

Shit. "You know about those?"

"Yep," he answered.

She was so screwed.

"I'll see you at eight on Saturday morning. *And* I'll be ready at six when you pick me up. But this is a whole lot of Dex for one weekend."

It didn't sound all that bad.

He laughed again.

His laugh didn't sound all that bad either.

Yep, she was screwed.

"I'll let you go to bed now. You start early in the mornings," he said.

"I'm already in bed," she blurted out.

He groaned. "Now I'll have that thought in my head all night."

She laughed. Then stopped. She couldn't believe she was laughing after having just been in tears.

"Dex?"

"Yeah, Honey?"

"Thanks for making me feel better."

"You're welcome. Good night, Kenna."

"Good night, Dex."

* * *

"Cut!"

"I thought we agreed those damned dogs were supposed to be boarded!" the director shouted at Rosalie.

Kenna was busy talking to the producer of this unadulter-
ated mayhem when she heard that asshole yelling at Rosalie.
She cut him off and started sprinting across the rose garden
ready to throat punch the guy who'd raised his voice at her
boss when she saw and heard something amazing. Buddy
Finch was nose-to-nose with the director.

"Get off the premises," Buddy roared.

"What?"

"You're so gone, today is a memory and tomorrow won't
even register."

"Who the hell are you?" the man sputtered.

"He's the man who can buy and sell you, and you've just
been sold," Kenna said as she came to a stop at Buddy's elbow.

The director looked at them with disdain. "This documentary is being funded by Mr. Shapiro's foundation."

"Exactly," Buddy said with satisfaction. "You just yelled at
the late Mr. Shapiro's widow."

"Her name is Rosalie Randall," he sputtered.

"That's her stage name," Kenna informed him.

"Ken, go apologize to Ms. Randall," the producer said as
he joined them.

"That won't cut it," Buddy said. "He's fired. Find another
director."

"Buddy, you can't mean that," the producer whined.

"I'll shut down this entire production. This documentary
doesn't have to be made," he ground out.

Kenna watched in amazement. This was not the easy-
going man she was used to seeing, but she liked it. It was

good to know that Rosalie's grandson could stand up for her so well. Rosalie was walking towards them with a smile on her face, it was obvious she had heard Buddy.

"Jim, you can't let this little shit walk all over you," the director said.

"It's done. You're fired. Get your things and go." The producer turned to a younger man who was standing close by. "Roy, you've just been promoted. Don't fuck up."

Five teacup poodles ran across the lawn, Smooches leading the way, followed by the maid.

"Smooches, bad girl," she yelled.

"I think the dogs would make an excellent addition to the documentary," Roy said to Rosalie.

"What a fucking suck-up," the original director muttered before he stomped away.

Kenna looked at Buddy who was fighting a grin.

"I wanted to talk to you, Kenna Dear," Rosalie said as she gripped her arm. Kenna allowed herself to be pulled towards the low stairs that led to the verandah.

"What did you need, Rosalie? Is there going to be a music video filming here next week? Is Beyoncé coming?"

"No, but Oprah magazine has approached me about an article and a photo shoot," Rosalie said as she sat down in one of the patio chairs. "I think we'll need to go to Sedona for that week. Will your mother be able to take care of Austin? Would you be able to get time off?"

"You're a hoot." Kenna laughed. "I never know what's next when I'm working with you."

"You needed some shaking up. Your life was too bland."

"I have work. I have Austin. It is good." Kenna looked at the chaos in the rose garden and thought that bland definitely had its good points.

"You've needed to get laid ever since I've known you."

Kenna's head whipped around in stunned disbelief. She knew that Rosalie wasn't a prude, but seriously?

"Seriously?"

"Yes, I said that, Honey. I'm surprised your girlfriends haven't taken you aside and laid down the law. So to speak." Rosalie chuckled at her double entendre.

Kenna's gut clenched. Jean had said that to her on numerous occasions.

"What, Honey?" Rosalie asked.

"It's Jean," Kenna whispered.

"Oh, I wasn't thinking," Rosalie leaned forward and patted her hand. "You've been holding up so well. Perhaps you should go home," Rosalie suggested.

"No, this is good. I need to take my mind off it."

She looked at Rosalie Randall, with her graceful sweep of white hair, and well-done makeup. The woman didn't look a day over seventy. Kenna shook her head. "Have I told you how much I love working for you?"

"Well, I hope it's more than that. I hope you love having me as a friend because that's what I consider you. I consider you my friend. And as your friend, I have to tell you, you need to get laid."

Kenna threw back her head and laughed. She couldn't

help it. She might not look ninety-two, but Rosalie Randall sure as hell looked regal as a duchess, and hearing her say that Kenna needed to get laid was pretty damned funny. Then to make matters worse, Rosalie arched one elegant eyebrow, and Kenna laughed even harder.

"Kenna, pull yourself together and listen to me."

She tried. She really did try. She pursed her lips together, clasped her hands in her lap and sat straight. "Yes?"

"I thought there was hope when you joined that dating site. That's why I had Buddy look into it. He cares about you like I do, so he aggressively bought out Lyle even when he didn't want to sell. After all that bother, we watched you, and you just sat there like a bump on a log. We could see how many men approached you. It showed that you were opening their e-mails, but you never responded. Then eight weeks ago, a miracle happened, and you responded! I've waited four years for the day to come that you actually showed interest in a man, talked to him, spent time with him. I'm ninety-two. I could die at any moment. You have to tell me how that dinner went!"

For just a second, Kenna was confused. What was Rosalie talking about, she and Dex weren't due to go out on their fancy date until this coming Saturday. Then she realized she was supposed to update her on last Saturday's dinner at her house. Damn, how had life gotten so confusing?

"Are you going to keep me waiting?" Rosalie demanded impatiently.

"After that heartfelt and dramatic performance? Of course not." Kenna grinned.

Rosalie gave her a considering look. "Was it Oscar worthy enough that you will tell me how the dinner went?"

Kenna leaned forward and took one of Rosalie's hands. "I love you."

"That's very nice dear. Now *talk!*"

"Mom made pot roast," Kenna began.

"Young lady," Rosalie said menacingly.

"Okay, okay. He brought flowers for my mom. She was over the moon. Gave me the look."

"What look?"

"The look that I had a good thing on the hook and I better not blow it."

Rosalie smiled. Apparently, she understood what she was talking about.

"What about Austin?"

"Austin took a bit longer to win over. First, did you know that Austin wants me to have a boyfriend? By the way, that word sucks! I never intend to date a boy." Kenna made a face.

"I don't think either you or Austin wants him calling the potential men in your life lovers..."

Kenna shuddered. "'Nuff said."

"Go on with your story."

"Even though Austin might want me to have a manfriend, he wasn't positive Dex was the guy. He had a lot of questions for him. Wanted to know where he went to college, what his degree was in."

"Was everything smooth sailing after that?"

"Mostly." Kenna went over to the mini fridge. "What can I get you?" she asked.

"Lemonade."

Kenna pulled out two bottles of sparkling lemonades, and then got glasses and poured. She handed Rosalie her glass.

"Austin actually asked Dex if he'd ever been married before. When he said no. Then he asked him if he had any kids. I thought Mom was going to choke on her potatoes."

"Buddy should have forwarded *him* the report. How did Dex handle the questioning?" Rosalie asked.

Kenna took a sip of her lemonade and her gaze warmed. "He took it great. He didn't talk down to Austin, he talked to him like an equal, and he didn't get frustrated. He made it part of the conversation. He asked Austin questions, too. I ended up finding out about Denny's girlfriend, and I didn't even know he had one."

"Sounds like he knows how to talk to kids."

"He's a natural," Kenna concurred. "Then Austin found out that Dex played baseball when he was at UNLV. That was even cooler then him being a SEAL if that was possible."

"Does Austin know what he wants to study? What he wants to be when he grows up?" Rosalie asked.

"Austin is a whiz when it comes to anything mechanical. Most of the kids he hangs out with like video games, he's the one who likes pulling apart the game counsel, or motherboard and dinking with it. He's been changing the oil on my car, and the spark plugs for the last three years. He said being a mechanic or a computer repair specialist won't allow him to take care of me in my old age, so he's going to become a mechanical engineer."

Kenna wiped the film off her glass of lemonade. The condensation looked like tears.

"Darling girl, what is making you sad?"

"Why would a fifteen-year-old boy be thinking of taking care of his mother in her old age? That is so wrong."

"You've raised a great son."

"Well he needs to be selfish," Kenna said vehemently. "If he wants to be a mechanic or a janitor, that's what he should do. I could care less about how much money he makes."

"Or a baseball player," Rosalie threw in.

"Yeah."

"Or a SEAL."

Kenna jerked her head. "Well, wait just a minute. They get hurt."

Rosalie laughed.

"Dinner went well?"

"Really well."

"Did Dexter kiss you?"

"Of course not."

"Why do you say it like that? He had you over at his townhome, didn't he? You're a beautiful woman. Are you saying he didn't kiss you then?"

"He didn't."

Rosalie looked so disappointed that Kenna immediately rushed to reassure her. "He flirted a lot."

"He did?"

"Yes."

"Did you like it?"

Kenna rolled her eyes. "Yes," she sighed. "He's annoying, but he's really funny."

"And handsome," Rosalie said slyly.

"Yes," Kenna agreed.

"You like him."

"Yes."

"You should go out with him again. Not just to visit those damn shelters," Rosalie said forcefully.

Kenna cleared her throat. She felt her face redden.

Rosalie set down her glass on the table and clasped her hands together. "You *are* going out together. You've been holding out on me."

"We have a date on Saturday. And then he's invited Mom, Austin, and me over to his place on Sunday for a barbeque."

"This couldn't be going any better than if a screenwriter wrote it," Rosalie enthused.

"As a matter of fact, he said to invite you."

Rosalie's eyes got wide. "I knew I liked that man. But that's just not possible. I have Buddy coming over for dinner on Sunday."

Kenna considered things for all of a second, but she knew that Dex had said he was inviting some of his team and their families over as well. "Have Buddy come as well. I was going to come pick you up, but this way he can drive you."

Rosalie clapped her hands. "Oh, Kenna! This will be so much fun."

The dogs must have heard the claps because they raced up the stairs and Kenna and Rosalie found themselves with laps full of poodles.

The maid came up carrying a bouquet of lilies. Rosalie held out her arms.

"No, Mrs. Randall, they are for Kenna," she said as she placed them on the table. Rosalie snatched up the card, a sparkle in her eye.

Kenna,
I'm sorry about your friend.
—T

"Who's T?" Rosalie asked.

Kenna sneezed, then sneezed again. Her eyes began to water.

"Are you allergic?" Rosalie asked.

Kenna nodded.

"Take these inside," Rosalie told the maid. She handed the card over to Kenna. "Do you know who 'T' is?"

"I don't know." Kenna sneezed again. "I'll ask around the hospital tomorrow. But it's weird they were delivered here."

The new director came bounding up the stairs. "Mrs. Randall, do you have time for us?" he asked sweetly. "Of course, we would love it if you would bring the dogs. The maid said you have a cat too, right?"

Kenna and Rosalie burst out laughing.

CHAPTER SEVEN

There had been no fights at the other missions, and Kenna's instincts had been right, no other facility needed money more than the Union Mission. On the drive between each place, she and Dex traded notes, and she was fascinated by the level of detail he took in at each shelter.

"I'll want to go back to each one and look at their computers. I know you're going to want to check out their financials, but I want to see how antiquated their systems might be."

"It won't be a problem at Lundquist, that place was slicker than snot," Kenna said. "They have the money rolling in."

"Yeah," Dex agreed. "Why did Rosalie have them on her list to begin with?"

"I'll have to ask her. But I think Herbert sniffs out money."

"I think you're right," he said as he turned into her driveway.

It was the middle of the day, but Dex got out of the car anyway and walked up with her to the front door. "Do you want to come in for something to drink?" She was flustered. "Iced tea, or water, or something?"

He stroked his finger along the side of her cheek as he smiled down at her. "Nope, just walking you to your door. All part of the service. I'll see you tonight at six."

She stood there dazed as she watched him get back into his jeep.

When she got into the house, it was empty.

She called her mom.

"Where are you guys?"

"I dropped Austin at Denny's. He's spending the night. I'm going to get my hair done."

"Mom, I'm not sleeping with Dex."

There was a pause. "Kenna Leigh, I did not think you were going to sleep with Dex. This is your first date with the man." She could hear the indignity in her mother's voice.

"It's our second date," she corrected.

"I don't care. I did not raise a daughter who would sleep with a man so soon."

"No, you didn't."

"She would wait until the third date."

Kenna choked out a laugh.

"You're nuts."

"I'm going to be late for my hair appointment. The gray is showing, and that mess needs to be cleaned up before to-morrow."

"Mom, I need a favor."

"What?"

"Can I text you pictures of dresses? I have to go to the mall and get something to wear for tonight. Dex says he's taking me someplace nice."

"What?" she shrieked. Kenna pulled the phone away from her ear. "You didn't tell me you had to go shopping. He's taking you someplace nice? Dress nice? Shit, Kenna. I'll get my hair done tomorrow morning. I'll meet you at the mall."

Kenna relaxed. Her mom was a great shopper, this would make her life so much easier. It would cost her more, but it would definitely be easier.

* * *

Thank God Austin wasn't here to see this. He'd know that she was nervous and cared. Plus, she needed to bury the dress in the closet so that her son never saw it.

She looked in the mirror again. She hadn't had time to go whole nine yards, but she'd used more than twenty dollars' worth of products thanks to her mother. Obviously, Miss Penny was holding out, because the woman knew beauty tricks.

"You want your hair to be touchable, so use this mousse, it smells good and will keep your hair in place," her mother had said.

The woman at the beauty supply store had picked out a shampoo and conditioner that would complement the mousse.

Hell, on the hair alone she was spending as much as she did on the shoes! And the shoes were gorgeous.

Kenna tugged on the straps of her electric blue form fitting dress and slipped on the silver sheened shoes. She turned to peer at the back of the dress, it fit perfectly. It was low, really low, but not too low. Her panties didn't show. Only because she'd bought really skimpy panties to wear with the dress. She took a deep breath.

"You can do this Kenna Leigh," she told herself.

She grinned. She looked good. Sexy even.

The doorbell rang. Her palms were sweating.

Get it together woman!

She smiled wide into the mirror. Perfect, no lip gloss on her teeth. She walked out of her bathroom and went downstairs.

One deep breath. She opened the door and stared.

Dex was wearing a suit. Navy blue of course. He was gorgeous!

"Um, hi. Would you like to come in?"

He didn't say anything, he just stood there.

"Dex?"

"You're a knockout."

"Would you like to come in?" she asked again.

"Where's Austin?"

"He's spending the night with a friend," she answered softly. "It was Mom's idea."

"I love your mother, but we need to go. Because if I come in, we're not leaving." His voice was low and husky, and she felt it all the way to her toes. "And I don't want that right now. I want an evening of torture."

"Torture?"

"Yeah. You. Wearing that dress. Wearing those shoes." He reached out and lightly caressed her hair. "Looking like you do, sitting next to me at dinner. That's the best kind of torture I can imagine, and I don't want to miss a minute of it."

Kenna couldn't help her smile. He hadn't seen the best part yet.

"Poppy, do you have a coat? It's supposed to get a little chilly later tonight."

She turned to get her jacket on the newel post and smiled when she heard his sharp intake of breath. She went back to him, and Dex's eyes were glittering like brown diamonds, as his hands reached for her coat.

He didn't say anything as he helped her into her jacket. Kenna looked up at him, and before she had a chance to say a word his mouth descended.

One warm hand reached beneath her coat and trailed down her naked back, and she moaned into his kiss. His tongue plunged, and all thought of her dress fled. She wound her arms around his neck, arching high to capture the taste of Dex Evans.

Hot, wet and carnal, the kiss was unlike any other in the history of the world. Up and down, his hand tracked a line of fire along her spine. His short hair was thick and silky under her fingers, and she loved the feel of it against her palm, but that quick thought splintered as his fingers raked through her curls and tugged, shards of sensation shot through her scalp. She loved the sting. It made her ache, made her want. Made her wet.

She bit his lip.

He groaned and pulled back.

"No," she pleaded.

"Are you for real?" he whispered.

"Hmm?"

Dex untangled his fingers from her glossy hair and cupped her cheek.

"You, Baby? Are you real? I'm about to go up in flames from just a taste. My control has never been this shaky."

Kenna kept staring up at him, trying to take in his words, but was more interested in watching his beautiful lips forming words.

"Are you listening to me?"

"I'm watching every word you're saying. You have a great mouth. Can I have it again?"

* * *

Dex barked out a laugh.

"God, Kenna, you're off the chain."

"I beg your pardon?"

Dex ignored her, and brought his mouth down, lightly touching his lips to hers. Just that little brush had him aching for more.

"Enough." He pulled away. "Kenna, you're powerful."

"It's not me. It's just the dress." He couldn't understand it; did she really have no idea about the power she wielded?

"If that's what you think, God help me when you realize the truth. Come on, let's get you into the jeep. We have reservations."

"Where are we going?"

"Pelican Bay."

"I've always wanted to go there," she said as she got out her keys to lock her door.

"Can I?"

She looked confused, then realized he was asking to lock her door for her. She handed him the keys with a smile. "I should teach that to Austin. It's nice."

She watched as he pocketed her keys. "And there goes the nice."

"What?" he asked.

"Aren't you going to give me my keys back? That'd be the nice thing to do."

"Aren't I going to unlock your door for you when we come back?" He watched her upper teeth bite at her lower lip. Again, he started to ache.

"Yes, I guess you would want to unlock my door."

"Ergo, I should have your keys."

"Did you just say, 'Ergo'?"

He draped his arm around her shoulders and guided her toward the passenger side of the jeep and helped her inside.

"Are you just looking for something to fight about? Save the fighting for after dinner so we can play make-up."

"You want to play with my make-up?" Her hazel eyes weren't twinkling. No, they were at half-mast and looking at him like she could eat him up with a spoon.

"Off the chain," he muttered. "Buckle your seat belt." When she fumbled, he brushed her hands away and clicked it in place. It wasn't a hardship getting close to those delectable curves.

"Is off the chain good?"

"According to Darryl, it is."

He shut the door and got into the driver's side. After they were on the road, she asked who Darryl was.

"He's my little brother. He got a scholarship to Cal State Fullerton."

"I didn't know you had a little brother. How much younger is he than you?"

Dex realized that he hadn't explained things correctly. "Darryl is part of the San Diego Big Brothers and Sisters program. He and I got paired up five years ago."

She didn't say anything after that, he looked over at her. She was looking off into the traffic.

"What are you thinking?" he asked.

"That's a pretty big commitment to make. What made you decide to do it?"

Shit, how did he answer that?

Time to pivot.

"A lot of the guys the teams I work with take on outside projects. Hunter Diaz, who you're going to meet at my place tomorrow, works with former gang members." He looked at her again as he took a turn towards Pacific Coast Highway.

"If you don't want to answer my question, just say so," she said quietly.

He'd forgotten how smart she was. Nothing got by her.

"Taking on Darryl was, and still is, a commitment that means a great deal to me. I'll tell you some other time why I decided to do it, okay?"

"Now was that so hard?" she asked with a genuine smile.

He blew out a breath. "No." And it really wasn't. She was easy to talk to. He asked her questions about Rosalie, and she answered them. Soon they were at the restaurant. He used the valet, so she wouldn't have to walk far in her heels.

It was chilly as they walked in, but as soon as they got to the hostess stand, Dex offered to take Kenna's coat. She gave him a demure smile, and he slipped it off. Seeing her long expanse of bare back that ended just above the swell of her ass had his mouth going dry. He walked behind her as they were led to their seats, but as he noticed all the heads turning, he moved closer, so that he was blocking the view. The show that Kenna was putting on was for *him*.

He'd asked for a table overlooking the ocean, and that's what they got. She sucked in her breath when they were seated.

"This place is gorgeous."

"I hear the food is good too," Dex said.

"You've never been here?"

"Nope, but Aiden has brought Evie."

She cocked her head, and he explained further. "Aiden is a teammate of mine. Evie's his fiancée."

"How many members are on your team?"

"Seven."

"Can I ask what you do?"

He liked that, she didn't just start peppering him with questions, she understood that some of what he did was classified.

"We all are multi-functional. But I specialize in communications and technology."

"That would make sense with your background."

"But the others are very adept."

"Have you worked together long?" She glanced up as the waiter handed them menus. They listened to the specials and placed their orders. Before long he found himself telling her about his team. She was fascinated to learn that his friend Griff had been on the Amtrak train that had crashed not far from San Diego.

"You guys lead interesting lives, even when you're not on assignment," she said as she took a small sip of wine.

"What about you? You haven't told me much more than what I've read in the profile. I take it your ex is out of the picture?"

Her hazel eyes darkened. "He was my high school boyfriend. I got pregnant when I was a senior. Both of our parents said we needed to get married. He had a partial scholarship in football, so he went to San Diego State. He blew it when he got caught cheating his sophomore year."

She pushed back her plate and took another delicate sip of wine.

"Then what happened?" he asked.

"He ended up going to a community college, and I needed to work more hours. But they wouldn't put me on full-time because they didn't want to pay benefits because I wasn't an accredited nurse's assistant, so I had to start picking up shifts at another home as well."

"Where was he working?"

"He wasn't."

"He was taking care of Austin?" Please say he was, Dex thought to himself.

"No, Mom was."

"What did your parents think of this?"

He watched as she smoothed her fingers over the silverware. "Dad died of a stroke the same year Austin was born. Caring for Austin was the way Mom coped. I was in too much of a daze about Dad's death and giving birth that I didn't realize I was in a bad situation."

Dex moved closer to her in the booth and put his arm around her shoulders. He was gratified when she snuggled closer. "Kenna, how long did this go on?" he asked softly.

"Jaden wasn't the best student in the world," she hedged.

"How long?"

"Austin was five when Jaden finally gave up. He got a job selling yellow pages advertising. He got a company car, and he had to go away a lot. The first three months he received a salary, but then it was mostly commission, and he hardly made anything. He'd come home late at night, and I could tell he'd been drinking. He got his first DUI six months after he started the job. He lost his job because he did it in the company car."

"How was it between the two of you?"

As she had told her story, she had been looking out over the ocean, but when he'd asked the question, she raised her eyes to look at him. "He didn't like me. Everything I did was wrong. He made me feel ugly and stupid."

Dex stroked her bare arm with his fingers. "But you got out of there."

"That's the pathetic part, Dex. I didn't. He left me."

"Thank God."

"You got that right," she said wanly. "But how pathetic was that, right?" She tried to shift away, but he was having none of it.

"Cut yourself some slack, you didn't know if you were coming or going. What would you say to anybody else in your shoes?"

She sighed. "I know. I know." She gave him a half-hearted grin.

"Now you're a registered nurse, and you've given your son a kick-ass life. I'd say you're a long way from pathetic. As a matter of fact, you're someone I admire."

She sucked in a deep breath and then gave him a brilliant smile. He couldn't help himself. He bent in for a kiss. It was perfect.

* * *

"He's looking like a very happy man," her mother observed as they watched Dex grill burgers and brats at the grill. "Did he spend the night?" she asked.

"Mother!"

"Damn. Here I cleared the decks and everything. I was sure with that dress that he wouldn't be able to resist." Penny giggled.

Kenna thought back to their good-night kiss on her sofa. It had been long and lush. Long and lush and wet. The man could kiss. But he had broken it off.

"Poppy, I so want more. I not only admire you; I desire you."

She was lying on top of him on the couch, and it was pretty damned obvious that he desired her.

"I'm a nurse, I'm trained to notice these things, Mr. Evans."

"But...I've agreed to a slower pace. This is only date number two. So, we're waiting."

"Hey! This is date number one," she said as she pressed up against his chest, grinding her lower half into his lower half. It felt glorious.

"Lunch at Danny's was date number one. We're waiting. You need time, and I'm enjoying the torture." His hand swept down her back and cupped her ass. His palm was warm and big, and she arched into it.

"Daughter, are you listening to me?"

Kenna shook her head and looked around noting Dex's backyard.

"Well, at least you saw some action." Her mother grinned. "I knew I could count on a Navy man." It was great to see her mother's eyes sparkling as she referred to her dad.

Kenna just raised one eyebrow and refused to comment, grateful when her son walked over, a half-eaten brownie in his hand.

"How many brownies does this make?" she asked.

"Only two. I'm saving room for a couple of cheese-burgers," he said. "I've been talking to Wyatt; did you know he surfs? He said he'd take me out sometime."

Kenna looked over at the sandy haired man who was standing next to Hunter Diaz. She kept saying their names in her head as she looked at each one of them so that she could memorize them.

"Austin, don't you think you have enough on your plate?"

Just then Wyatt looked their way and grinned, obviously knowing what Austin was asking. He put his palms together in a praying motion. The man was charming.

"Let me talk to him," Kenna said. "I'm not promising anything."

Austin smirked. He knew he'd won.

Damned smart kid.

"Food's up," Dex called out.

Kenna watched as Penny and Griff's wife Miranda uncovered the side dishes and condiments. They were soon sitting at various places around the backyard. Dex and Hunter had brought out the dining room table from inside to accommodate more seating. Rosalie was having a grand time entertaining Evie and Aiden. She saw Buddy and Dex deep in conversation and wondered what was going on and then realized that both of them had technical backgrounds. She wandered over to join them.

"Lyle Gale was less than happy, but he has an appalling reputation, so I didn't mind using certain methods to acquire the dating website."

Dex chuckled. "You did this all for Rosalie?"

"My grandmother is a force to be reckoned with." Buddy looked over at Kenna. "Keeping watch over her protégé was a pleasure. But I wouldn't have done any of this if it hadn't made good business sense."

"Actually, that makes me feel a whole hell of a lot better," Kenna said with a sigh of relief.

Buddy smiled at her.

"I'm hoping you can do me a favor Kenna, dear." It was funny how he talked to her like she was his daughter when he was five years younger than her. "I have to go to the office this afternoon. Could you take Grandmother home? I don't want her to miss any of the festivities, she's having a great time."

He leaned forward and gave her a kiss on the cheek, then shook Dex's hand. "I'm glad she found you, Man. We'd given up hope." Buddy grinned.

Buddy left through the sliding glass door.

"Let me get you a plate of food," Dex said. "I think Evie's starting to tell her stories to Rosalie. This ought to be good."

* * *

The night was winding down. Despite the fact that her son had eaten far more brownies and cookies than she wanted to think about, dessert was now being served. Penny had just brought out a Bundt cake, and Kenna was going inside and get something to cut it with. As she opened the sliding glass door, she heard the distinctive ring of her phone and went to her purse.

Austin was getting ice cream of the freezer when she answered the phone.

"I've been calling for over an hour, what took you so long?"

She didn't answer. She was frozen.

"Kenna, did you like the flowers?" he prompted.

"Who is this?" But she knew who it was. She recognized that creepy, raspy voice.

"I've e-mailed Mary Poppins many times, but you didn't reply. I had to get your attention."

Ice slithered down her spine. "How did you get my number? How did you know where to send me flowers?" Her voice rose.

The phone was taken from her hand, hazel eyes blazed at her.

"Who are you?" Austin demanded of the caller.

"Answer me!"

"Answer me!"

Austin looked at the phone in his hand and turned to Kenna. "What was that about?"

"What do you mean 'what was that about'?" She snatched the phone back from her son and looked at the number. It said it was unidentified. Dammit. "What the hell were you doing, taking the phone out of my hand?" she demanded.

"You were upset."

She put it up to her ear again, but the caller had hung up.

She looked up at her son. He had acted like a protector. She got a melty feeling in the pit of her stomach.

Austin slid open the sliding glass door. "Dex!" Austin called out.

All melty feelings faded.

"Yo!"

"Come here," Austin yelled.

Dex came inside. Austin did a chin tilt, and Dex closed the door. Seriously. What the hell? They were communicating with chin tilts?

"Mom just got a crank call that totally flipped her out. Apparently, he's even sent her flowers."

Two sets of eyes turned on her.

"Kenna, what the hell is going on?" Dex asked.

"I've been getting hang-ups, and lately they've turned to actual calls," her voice trailed off.

"What's this about flowers?" Dex questioned, his voice hard.

"I got flowers sent to me at Rosalie's house." She bent to her purse and pulled out the card that had come with the flowers. "I've been asking around at the hospital, trying to figure out who had sent them. I knew it wasn't you because you're not a 'T.' Your middle name is Anthony." She paused and looked at Dex, her eyes widening. "Shit, I didn't think. You don't go by Tony, do you?"

"How did you know my middle name was Anthony?" he demanded.

"Buddy ran a report on you."

There was a long pause as Dex assessed her. "Okay, we'll table that for a later date. No, I don't go by Tony. In the meantime, we'll talk about the fact that you've been getting calls and flowers from somebody, and you haven't told me or the police."

"Why would I do that?" she asked, confused.

"I don't know," he said sarcastically. "Maybe because one of your good friends was just murdered?"

Kenna gulped. Shit. She hadn't considered that.

"This is probably just some whackjob," she hedged.

"My point exactly." Dex's voice was grim.

She opened her mouth again to disagree and then saw her son's white face.

Damn. Shit. Fuck.

She bent again to her purse and pawed through it until she found Detective Warren's card. "I'm going to call the detective who spoke to me about Jean. I'm so sorry I didn't think to do this before," she said looking at Austin.

Austin gave a slight nod.

She got the detective's voice mail. She left a brief message. "It's Sunday, I'm sure he'll get back to me tomorrow morning," she assured the two glowering males.

"Mom, he knows Rosalie's address," Austin said quietly. "That means he knows our address."

It did. It so did.

"Austin, we have no way of knowing if Jean's murder and these crank calls are connected. We need to chill," she put her hand out to touch his shoulder, but he jerked away.

"Austin. If there is a connection, this is actually some good news. The police will have some leads to track down with the phone calls and the flowers," Dex said calmly. She threw him a grateful look for keeping things calm with her son.

"In the meantime, we'll stay with your grandmother tonight. How about that?" she offered.

She saw the look of intense relief on her son's face and felt better.

"That sounds good, Mom."

"Go grab a cheeseburger before Dex's friends eat them all," she suggested.

"Do you have this?" Austin asked Dex.

What the hell did that mean?

"Yeah, we'll get this locked down. You better grab the food before Wyatt nabs everything," Dex gave her son another reassuring smile.

Austin nodded and picked up the tub of ice cream and headed out.

Kenna turned to Dex. "When did the two of you get so chummy?"

"A common interest made us fast friends."

"What's that supposed to mean?" Kenna demanded.

"Since you don't take your well-being seriously, Austin and I needed to team up." Why did Dex seem even taller and wider than normal?

"Why would he turn to you?"

"You're kidding, right? Your son has probably already googled me. He knows which way the wind is blowing."

"Googled." That reminded her. "Damn. I need to explain about Buddy's report. Look, he was just making sure that you were a good guy."

"I don't give a shit about that." He was angry. "What were you thinking not calling the police or at the very least mentioning this to me?"

"Huh? Why would I have mentioned it to you?" Now he was just confusing her.

"Weren't the calls bothering you? Making you feel uncomfortable?"

"Well sure," Kenna admitted.

"You should have told me about them."

"Why on God's good green earth would I have done something like that?" She put her phone and Detective Warren's card back in her purse and tucked it back by the chair near the sliding glass door.

"Because I handle problems," he said. His face had a hard expression.

"We've been on two dates. We've talked on the phone a few times. I haven't even told my mom about this. I'm sure as hell not going to tell some guy I barely know about some creepy phone calls."

At her words, she watched his face go through a magical transformation.

"Poppy, we've been communicating for almost two and a half months."

"Two months," she immediately countered.

"Okay two months. But you have to admit I'm someone more than you barely know."

"Fine, a few e-mails, a couple of phone calls and two dates."

"And you've had me investigated."

She felt like stomping her foot. "Don't make this some sort of game."

"God, Kenna, the last thing I want to do is make this a game. Someone is already fucking with your head. I'm trying to support you. I want to be someone you can lean on."

"I don't believe in that," she said loudly. Really loudly.

Fuck, had those words just come out of her mouth?

God, she was mortified.

Dex looked over his shoulder to the backyard. A couple of heads had turned their way. He picked up her purse and pulled her further into the house to his office and shut the door. Dex opened his arms.

"What are you doing?"

"I want to give you a hug, Poppy. You need one."

Kissing him was one thing, but taking a hug from him when she so desperately needed one? No way. Nuh Uh. Not going there.

"Kenna, come here. I promise I won't let you down." She looked into sincere brown eyes. Soulful. Kind. Compassionate. Kenna hesitated. Just this once she wanted a man like her father that she could trust and lean on. Please don't let her be wrong.

She stepped into his arms, and he enveloped her. His hand cupped the back of her head, and he kissed her hair.

"Talk to me, Baby."

"It's stupid. I haven't really been all that scared until you pointed out Jean was murdered. I've just put it down to some creep, ya know?" Her voice was muffled against his chest, and his arms clutched her tighter.

"I'm sure it *is* just some creep, and the two things aren't re-lated at all," he whispered.

She pushed away from his chest to look him in the eye. "You're just saying that to make me feel better, aren't you?"

"Yep," he nodded.

"Don't do that Dex. I'm a big girl, I put on big girl panties, I can handle the truth."

"What kind of panties? I'm partial to thongs."

She laughed. How could she be laughing? She hit his chest. Hard. He caught her fist and kissed her knuckles.

"Big girl panties mean granny panties," she explained.

"I'm not partial to those." His lips feathered over the back of her hand, then he uncurled her fist, and pressed a kiss to her palm. She shuddered. "I think I'm going to make a stop at Victoria's Secret for you," he said.

"Goddammit, stay on track. We were discussing the fact that you were lying to me to make me feel better." That was twice in twenty minutes she felt like stomping her foot. What, was she five?

"Kenna, I'm not going to make any kind of guess. What's the point? Let's wait and see what the experts say, okay?"

He hugged her closer. She shut her eyes and melted into his warmth.

"Okay."

* * *

He arranged for Griff to take Rosalie home, then he followed Kenna and Austin to their house to pack. He helped them unload at Penny's house and kissed Kenna goodnight afterwards he headed home where he hit his computer. He placed a call to Detective Warren, told him to call him first thing in the morning, if not fucking sooner. Then he went to work.

He had three pieces of information to go on. The unidentified callers coming into her cell phone. The flowers. The fact that the caller had referred to her as Mary Poppins. He was going to leave the first two things to the cops, the flowers were going to take a lot of legwork. The call was going to take hacking into the wireless company, and that would take time. Right now, he already had a way into the dating site, so that's where he would start.

"I'm going to find you, you motherfucker."

CHAPTER EIGHT

Dex joined Kenna on Monday afternoon when she met with the detectives about the case. He had caught her look of surprise when he'd arrived at the police station. She needed to start getting used to things. Yep, even in such a short amount of time, she was pretty damned important to him. She was special. He hadn't met that many special people in this lifetime. She shone. Thinking of how she was with Austin was a miracle after what he'd witnessed in Egypt. She deserved this kind of care from him.

Warren and Sanchez seemed to know what they were doing. They didn't share a lot about what was going on with Jean's case since it was an ongoing investigation, but it was obvious they had someone in their sites.

"Ms. Wright, there was someone in Ms. Baldwin's life who is of particular interest. We are currently closing in on him. This has nothing to do with the dating site, so the fact that your caller mentioned your dating profile name suggests these are two different men," Detective Warren said.

"Thank God. That means I can stay at home tonight." Kenna said.

"How sure are you that you have the right guy?" Dex asked.

"We need a few more days to make our case and get a search warrant, but it's looking good," Sanchez said.

"Good enough that Kenna shouldn't worry?" Dex asked.

Sanchez leaned forward across the interview table. "Ms. Wright, you are being stalked. It's not a good sign that somebody has your phone number and your employer's address. We're homicide detectives. This isn't our purview. We'll get your set up with someone who can take a report."

"What good will taking a report do?" Dex demanded. "Will they track down who sent the flowers? The telephone calls?"

Both detectives looked uncomfortable. Kenna looked at them, then at Dex. "Don't worry, this is some kind of weird stalker who's just into me. It's not a murderer."

Dex turned to the detectives. "This is more than a stalker, isn't it? He's gone to a lot of trouble to learn a lot about Kenna. Doesn't this shit normally escalate?"

"If it is somebody in her past, like an ex, then yes, it does. If it is just a crazy, then they can find a new target. You can't predict crazy," Warren said. "But seriously, this isn't the murderer." He turned back to Kenna. "Ms. Wright, we'll get you in touch with someone in our department who specializes in this, and you'll need to keep them informed. If you're approached, they'll up their investigation, and you'll be able to get a restraining order."

Kenna smiled. "I'm just thankful I don't have to worry about a murderer. A stalker I can handle."

Dex saw red. To his way of thinking there was not one damn thing to be thankful for. He'd culled the dating site the previous night and found that Kenna had received over a thousand e-mails. It amazed him that for some reason she had replied to his profile. It made him uncomfortable since it hadn't even been an e-mail he'd written. Granted the picture had been his, and the basic facts about his life. But still, the woman had been inundated, how in the hell had he made the cut?

He went with her when she made out her report to the police officer. The cop was sympathetic, but she explained there wasn't much she could do at this point. She gave Kenna her card and told her to keep her informed if she was contacted again.

"At least I don't have to stay at Mom's tonight," Kenna said as they stepped into the San Diego sunlight.

"Was it really that much of a hardship?" Dex asked as he walked her to her car.

"I like having my own space. Austin ends up sleeping on the pull-out sofa in the living room, and I hate that for him."

"You would."

"What does that mean?"

"It means you're a good mother." Dex opened her car door.

"Do you have a problem with that?"

"Hell no. I think it's sexy."

She gave him a confused look.

"I've seen shitty mothers. Fuck, I've seen absolute monsters. Seeing someone who is so into her kid is like seeing sunshine."

Kenna smiled wide.

"That's got to be the nicest thing anybody has ever said to me."

"Well stick around, I've got a lot of nice things to say to you. Unfortunately, we're doing some maneuvers for the next few nights so I won't be able to ask you out. Promise me that you'll get someone to walk you to and from your car at night when you leave the hospital?"

She gave him an exasperated look. He stared down at her. Eventually, he won.

"All right, I promise."

"If I say, 'good girl,' how will you respond?"

"Do you want to be kneed in the nuts?"

He chuckled and cupped her cheeks. He kissed her. Soft. Kenna responded. Sweet.

He lifted his head. "What was that for?" she asked.

"I get turned on by being threatened."

"I'll remember that. I like being kissed by you," she admitted.

He liked that. Straight up. She just said what she thought.

"Normally, I love spending time with the team, but not this time. I won't be calling either," he frowned.

"That's all right."

"No, it's really not." He made a decision. "Kenna, I'm going to drop by the hospital in a couple of hours with a friend of mine. I want you to meet him so that you'll know who you can reach out to while I'm out of touch."

"I thought you said your team would be with you."

"He's on one of the other teams. He's a good guy. You'll like him."

"Dex, isn't this over kill? I mean the cops don't think this is a big deal."

"Let me do this, okay?" He stroked her cheek with his thumb.

"Okay."

* * *

They grew all of the SEALs big. But it was hysterically funny to see this big man squirm around and look as guilty as her son did when he didn't finish his homework. Dex had introduced him as Clint Archer, the man who had played the practical joke on him with the dating site. He was also going to be her go-to guy if anything odd came up while Dex was on maneuvers for the next four nights.

"I'm not sure how comfortable I feel with Clint," Kenna said quietly. Truthfully, she felt fine, but it was fun putting the wood to the man. It was clear he hadn't thought his joke through, he had only regarded it from Dex's point of view, not from the women's. Kenna relished the idea of making him feel just a little bit bad.

"Ma'am, my wife couldn't make it. But if she had you'd see that she has already kicked my ass all the way to Tijuana and back for this prank. If you ever call me and I need to be at your house, it's more than likely that she'll come with me. You'll like her, and the two of you can rake me over the coals together."

"Don't listen to him, Kenna. He's just playing that up in hopes that I won't retaliate," Dex said.

The three of them were sitting in the hospital cafeteria.

"No, I'm not," Clint protested. "Hell Dex, Lydia will probably help you concoct whatever kind of retribution you have in mind. She said that playing with the hearts and minds of women crossed a line." He looked across the table at Kenna. "I understand why you don't trust me." Clint gave Kenna a sincere look. "It looks like something good might be happening out of this, but still, I screwed up. In the meantime, you're going to have to allow me to back you up while Dex isn't around."

Damn, she really liked the man. Kenna smiled. Time to take him off the hook.

"I trust you just fine. Dex speaks highly of you. Personally, I think the joke was pretty funny...in retrospect. Dex was really nice about it, the way he replied to each woman."

She saw Clint fight back a grin. Yep. It was almost like dealing with her son and his friends. Suddenly his demeanor changed.

"Dex tells me that you've promised you won't be taking any unnecessary chances while he's away."

"Huh?" She looked between the two men. "What are you talking about?"

"Kenna, you promised you would be walking to and from your car with someone."

"That was when we thought it was the murderer..." her voice trailed off as both men shook their heads at her.

"No. You have a stalker. At all times, you are on alert. That means when it is dark, you do not walk to your car by yourself, are we clear?" Dex was deadly serious. Who was this man, and what had happened to the easy-going guy she was used to?

"Isn't this overkill?"

Both men stared at her, there was no give in either face. "Fine." She sighed. "I promise."

"The minute you are contacted by this whackjob, you contact Clint first, then the police. Hand Clint your cell phone, okay?"

"Why?"

"He's going to look at a couple of things that will allow him to track the caller the next time they call."

"What's your password?" Clint asked her when she handed him her phone.

She hesitated.

Dex looked at her. "Honey, normally it would be me doing all of this, I just don't have time. I have to check in at noon. Clint could do everything he plans to do without your knowledge and without your password, but we're trying to be upfront with you."

"What all are you planning to do?" she asked them.

"He's going to monitor your calls from unidentified callers," Dex explained.

Clint looked up. "Kenna, if he calls, try to keep him on the line so that I can pinpoint his location, okay?"

"Just like on TV. Okay."

"Also, Clint is inserting a tracking device so we can find you."

"Oh, I have that on Austin's phone," Kenna smiled.

"We'll have you set up with the rest of the women of Midnight Delta," Clint said.

"Midnight Delta?" Kenna asked.

"That's Clint's SEAL team. Mine is Black Dawn," Dex explained. "Obviously, Black Dawn is the better team."

Clint coughed as he took a sip of coffee. It sounded a lot like he said the word 'bullshit.' She grinned at the two man/boys.

"Why are you putting tracking on my phone?" she asked.

"For my piece of mind," Dex said.

"Yep, that sounds like why I arranged it with Austin. But seriously, it makes sense between Austin and me, but not for you and me."

Dex pushed up from the booth. "Kenna, can you come take a walk with me?"

"Huh?" She looked up at Dex, as he towered over her and then looked across the cafeteria table to Clint who was busy staring at her phone.

"Kenna, come outside with me for a second. I want an opportunity to bask in second hand smoke."

That about summed it up she thought as they walked out of the cafeteria, down the hall, and outside past the group of smokers.

"What did you want to talk about? Because Dex, I don't think I need you tracking me. Sure, checking my phone for the unidentified caller fine, but the tracking me I just don't get," she said as he brought her to a halt in a small alcove near the parking garage.

"Let me explain it to you." He speared his fingers through her hair, whisking the scrunchie into the bushes. His head descended, blocking out the California sun and she sank into the wonder of his kiss.

All higher-level thought fled as the sumptuous feel of his lips devouring hers took over her mind, her body, her soul. It was her toes that finally got through to her. She was standing on them, and they got cramped. Her eyes fluttered open, and she looked at Dex. Her insides melted. The look on his face was incredible. His eyes opened, and his head lifted just a little.

"Did that help explain things?" he asked softly.

She nodded her head. "But I would love it if you'd kiss me again."

"First the words Babe. I'm staking my claim. As such, your safety is paramount. You have a whackjob after you, so I want to make sure I can get to you if you need help. If I'm not around, I want the best of the best to be there in my place. That's Clint and his guys. You got me?"

"What answer gets me another kiss?"

Dex's smile shone brighter than the California sun. "I like that you're a smartass."

"You didn't answer my question. Nor am I being kissed." She pulled at his neck.

"Poppy, did you hear me?"

"I heard that you're going to be gone for four days. I heard that you need to be at the base by noon. I want my kiss."

Dex's eyes went dark when he saw she was serious. "Did I say I like that you're a smartass?"

She nodded.

"I like that you are the most upfront woman I have ever met. No games. No artifice. Just you. You are amazing." His fingers splayed out against her jaw, and his thumb teased her bottom lip. "God Kenna, I so owe Clint."

This kiss was different. Just as lush, but flavored with tenderness and magic. Kenna floated in his arms suffused with joy. When she felt tears beginning to form, she looked up at him and scowled.

"What?"

She hit him on his chest with the flat of her hand. Hard.

"What did I do?" he asked again.

"That's for starting to make me care."

CHAPTER NINE

It was Saturday morning, and she was at Lundquist House on University Avenue in San Diego. Kenna had a toddler on her hip and was talking to the child's mother.

"They're going to help me find an apartment," she was explaining.

Kenna was trying to pay attention, but her phone wouldn't stop vibrating. It was making her purse shake. She should have just turned the damned thing off, but she always worried that Austin or her mom might need her.

"Excuse me, I need to check my phone, it might be my son."

The young woman smiled and took her son from Kenna's arms.

The display said, unidentified caller. It was probably the whack job, but still, it could be from one of Austin's friends, or it could be an emergency *about* Austin. She had to answer.

"Hello?"

"Mary Poppins, it's about damned time you picked up!" This time the raspy voice was loud. But it still slithered. He was disguising it.

Her thumb hovered over 'END,' when she realized Dex and Clint had told her to keep the creep talking.

She stepped away from the girl and her baby and whispered into the phone. "What do you want from me? Who are you?"

"Don't play coy with me. You think just because you're beautiful you can ignore a man." Now he was quiet and scary. They'd been right, the guy was a serious whackjob.

"Look, Dude, I ignored everybody who e-mailed me. Don't take it personally."

"You didn't. You're seeing the sailor."

"How do you know?" Kenna saw the girl's head jerk up. She needed to take it down a notch. "How do you know who I'm spending time with?" she asked in a quieter voice.

"I know a great deal about you. I wish I could get as close to you as Smooches does. I like to cuddle." The last was said with a grating laugh.

Kenna didn't respond. She couldn't. How could he know the name of Rosalie's dog? Who was this guy? Oh God. Austin.

"Stay away from me."

"You get it now, don't you? You're worried about your son. Don't be. I care about you, Kenna. I wouldn't hurt your child.

I want you to like me. Now if you do something to make me angry..." he let the words hang out there.

"Stay away from Austin. You stay away from my boy!" Out of the corner of her eye, she could see the little boy was now crying.

"Or what?" the man asked softly.

"I'm calling the police."

"They couldn't help Jean." The man laughed. It was the evilest sound Kenna had ever heard in her life.

The line went dead.

* * *

Herbert Lundquist was standing over her in his office. She had just gotten done making phone calls ensuring that Austin was safely at Denny's house for the rest of the weekend. She'd also convinced her mother to stay with her bridge partner Wilma until Monday.

"I'll have my assistant drive you to the police station," Herbert said.

"I'm fine to drive myself," Kenna said.

"Please, beg my pardon, but you didn't look well a half hour ago. I think you need someone to drive you."

There was a knock on the door, and then Clint Archer walked into the office.

"Kenna, we have a problem," Clint said at the same time as Lundquist asked, "Who is this?"

"I know. He called me. He threatened my son."

"Hello, Mr. Lundquist." Clint walked up to Herbert. "My name is Clint Archer. I'm providing security for Ms. Wright until her boyfriend arrives home this afternoon. Could you give the two of us a moment of privacy?"

"Kenna, is this all right?" Herbert asked her.

Kenna nodded.

As soon as the door closed, Clint turned on her. "Lady, what is your problem?"

"He threatened my son."

"Why didn't you call me as soon as your call with that fucker ended? I called you Kenna. You saw my number come up on your phone and you ignored it. What the hell?"

"You saw the call come in. You had the tracking device, hell you probably listened in. You knew everything, Clint. I trusted you to do your part. I didn't have time to take your call, I had to make sure Austin and mom were okay!" She was shaking.

"When you weren't taking my calls, what were you doing?" he demanded.

Kenna explained exactly what was said, and then told Clint how she'd arranged for Austin to stay at his best friend's house for the weekend.

"God save me from amateurs," Clint said looking up at the ceiling. Then he looked down at his watch. "Just two and a half hours and I'm off duty."

"What are you talking about? I took care of everything," Kenna asked, confused. She started toward the door; Clint stepped in front of her. He ran his hand through his hair.

"Point one, you agreed to call me as soon as the whackjob called you again. You didn't. Then when I tried to call you, you didn't answer. When I tracked you to this place, they wouldn't put me through to you, they said you were in a conference with Lundquist. I hauled ass to get over here. I knew Austin had been threatened, I wanted to come up with a game plan with you. If you had called me or taken my call, I could have picked him up immediately and gotten him someplace more secure than his friend's house. Let's face it, if this whackjob knows the name of Rosalie's teacup poodle, there is a good chance he knows about Austin's best friend, Denny."

Fear slammed into her. She couldn't take in air. She opened her mouth to speak, but nothing would come out. He was right.

Clint saw the problem and put his hands gently on her shoulders. "Let's get into my truck and go pick up your son from Denny's house, okay?"

She nodded. It was all she could do.

* * *

"Who owns this place again?" she asked Dex.

"Jack Preston and his wife Beth normally live here. They're visiting his folks in San Antonio for ten days, so we're staying here."

"And he's a SEAL? Just how much do you guys make?" she asked as she opened the Sub-Zero refrigerator.

Dex smiled. It was the first sign her sense of humor was returning. When he had arrived back from maneuvers, Kenna had been a mess. He didn't know whether to thank Clint or punch him for scaring the bejesus out of his girlfriend.

It had been Clint's idea to ask Jack to use his house. They'd arrived five hours ago. Austin had eaten half of the fridge's contents, and Penny had sucked down almost a whole bottle of wine, so both of them were now in bed. At last, he had Kenna alone, and he wanted to take her emotional temperature.

"Jack comes from money. A few years back he invited me and some of the other guys from our team to his ranch in Texas. It's a huge operation."

Kenna went back to putting dishes in the dishwasher.

"You can leave the dishes for tomorrow. I'll do those when I get back from taking you to work. I have the next couple of days off."

"I like doing dishes, it's soothing," she said as she rinsed off another plate. He noticed she was taking pains not to look at him.

"Kenna, talk to me."

"I don't want to talk. I want to do something normal. I want to do something that doesn't include taking phone calls from psychos, being lectured by your friends, having to talk to the police or moving out of my house, okay?" Her voice raised at the end as she slammed a mug into the dishwasher rack.

Dex winced. "Kenna, I think we need to discuss what the police said."

She shoved another glass in the rack. "No, we don't."

As she grabbed a bowl off the counter, he tugged it out of her hands. She finally met his eyes. "I don't want to talk. If I talk, I'm afraid I'll fall apart, and my mom and my son need me to keep my shit together."

He grasped both of her hands, and pulled her out of the kitchen, into the small sitting room that had a loveseat. He sat and drew her down close beside him.

"Dex, I told you I didn't want to talk."

"Then don't talk, just rest here for a little bit."

Her stiff body eventually began to relax into his, then her head tipped up so that she could look into his eyes. "I'm scared."

He nodded for her to continue.

"When Sanchez told me that they were wrong about who they'd thought the killer was, it scared the hell out of me. Especially when they said they think my calls could be coming from the same guy."

Dex wasn't scared, he was enraged. He'd called Detective Warren before he'd left on maneuvers and given him Clint's name and number. He'd specifically said that if anything changed in the investigation, Warren needed to call Clint so that he'd have a heads up on ensuring Kenna's safety. Warren had known for twenty-four hours that they'd had the wrong guy. He and Sanchez should have called Clint. They didn't.

That meant for the last twenty-four hours Kenna had been left unprotected.

"What are you thinking, Dex?"

"I'm thinking how good dinner was tonight. I liked the meatloaf you cooked."

"Bullshit. You're still pissed off. I can feel it rolling off you in waves," she said as she pushed away from him.

"Come back here. I was thinking of meatloaf and cuddling."

She was studying him closely. He knew he wasn't getting away with anything. Still, her next words stunned him. "Your protective instincts are so deep, they're in the marrow of your bones. What happened to you? What made you that way?"

"It's what SEALs do," he said glibly.

"Fine, don't answer me." She deserved a better answer. She deserved more. She deserved the truth.

Slowly, as if the words were torn from him, he said, "I couldn't save him." Even now, after all these years, his voice got thick just thinking about Ricky.

"Who?" she asked softly.

"My brother."

She reached out and brushed her hand over his heart. Then kept it there. He pressed his hand on top of hers, holding it close. Needing it close. Needing *her* close.

"Ricky was older than me. He...he was everything to my parents. They thought the Earth orbited around him. I came eight years after Richard Edward Evans was born. I was an accident. They'd only wanted one child, so they didn't give me any attention, but Ricky did. He had my back from the day I was born. I might not have been wanted by Mom and Dad, but I knew that Ricky loved his baby brother."

Dex pictured his brother in his mind's eye. He liked thinking of him when he was sixteen. Whole and healthy. Ready to take on anything.

He looked down and saw Kenna's empathetic and confused expression. "You can't even wrap your head around it, can you?"

"I can understand Ricky loving you and having your back," she said slowly. "But your parents? No. I don't get that in the slightest."

Dex sighed. He still didn't get it either. It just was.

"What happened?" she asked.

"He was popular, and the parents gave him everything he wanted. They never said no to anything. Cars, vacations with his friends during the summer, anything he asked for. He was just a kid, but our mom came from money, and they never denied him anything. Whenever Ricky was gone, they'd send me to Gram and Gramps here in San Diego."

"And?"

"When I got back the summer before his senior year, he'd changed. I was nine. All of a sudden, he didn't have any time for me. It hurt. When I tried to talk to him, he yelled at me and told me to quit following him around like a goddamn shadow." Dex remembered that moment like it was yesterday. They'd been in the backyard, and Ricky had screamed at him.

"It was then that I knew something bad was going on. The Ricky I knew and loved would never have said that to me."

"What did you do?"

"I spied on him. I caught him shooting up in his bedroom. I didn't know it was heroin, I just knew it was drugs because I'd seen it on cop shows, so I knew it was bad. I told Mom and Dad, but Ricky denied it, and they didn't believe me. They grounded me for telling lies."

"There had to have been signs. Didn't they take it seriously? Why would a nine-year-old boy lie about a thing like that?" She was appalled.

"Because he was their golden boy," Dex sighed.

"If they loved him, they needed to take notice," she protested.

"It didn't work that way with them, Poppy," he said sadly.

"What'd you do next?"

Dex smiled. She knew him. She totally got the fact that he hadn't given up. "I snuck into his room and found his stash. There were needles and everything he needed to shoot up. He had it hidden in his sunglasses case. I brought that to my parents."

"And then?"

"Hell Kenna, I could see how mad they were at me. Somehow in their minds, I was the bad guy. When Ricky told them it was his friend's drugs, they immediately believed him. That was when they arranged for me to be sent to boarding school."

She ripped her hand away from his chest and used both hands to cup his face. "Oh, Dex. What happened next, Honey?"

"Ricky wouldn't talk to me. I begged him, but he just froze me out. I was packed up and sent away within forty-eight hours. Two weeks later, I was attending his funeral. He'd overdosed."

Her hazel eyes were swimming with tears.

"I'd fucked up. I didn't keep him alive."

"No, Honey, no. You were a child, you can't actually think that."

"When I got to the funeral and saw Gramps, I lost it. I don't know how I didn't think to call him. Even now I don't know how I could have been so stupid not to have called him. He would have fixed it."

"What did your grandfather say when you said that to him?"

"He said that they wouldn't have listened to him either."

"You see?"

"But they would have," Dex said stubbornly.

She stroked his jaw. "You're looking at this from the eyes of a nine-year-old. Look at it today. You still know your parents. Look at them now. Could the man you are today convince them or are they the type of people who only see what they want to see?"

Dex paused. After he turned eighteen, he'd rarely spoken to his mother and father. But the few times he had seen them, he realized that they were totally self-absorbed. Even his dad said barely one word to his own parents. It hurt Gram and Gramps, but they tried not to show it. There was something missing in his mom and dad, the only love they'd had to give had dried up once Ricky had died.

"Honey?" she prompted.

He looked down at her and gave a slight smile. "You're right, I couldn't convince them of anything. They live in their own little world." His voice went hoarse. "It just breaks my heart that I lost him like that."

She rested her head against his chest, under his chin. "He's still with you. He's always with you. It's why you do what you do with Darryl. It's why my son admires you so much. You take the love you have for your brother, and you spread that around, and he watches you do it."

Dex closed his eyes. He could see it. What she said made perfect sense, it was as if a dark cloud had lifted, and peace filled him.

But enough was enough. The corner of his mouth ticked up just a little. It was time to get back to cuddling. Maybe even canoodling.

"You're full of shit," he said to her.

She shoved up and scowled at him. "I so am not. I was being spiritual and wise." Then her eyes lit up, she caught on to his new mood.

He pulled her back against him, swinging her legs over his so she was resting in his lap. "Okay Miss Wiseone, tell me what's on my mind right now."

Kenna put her fingers against her temples. "Dexter Anthony Evans is thinking he is being charming and can maybe get to second base."

"Wrong."

"I am not wrong." Kenna's eyes were dancing.

"Third. I'm thinking I can get to third base."

"Not next to the kitchen. My son gets up in the middle of the night to snack. There will be no baserunning for you."

Dex laughed. How in the hell did she manage to make him laugh? He never did after the specter of Ricky came up. "You so *are* Mary Poppins. You have magic just like she does."

Kenna looked bewildered, and that was an adorable look for her. He hugged her closer.

"You do, Kenna. I have never come close to feeling as good and as happy as I do when I'm with you."

"I don't know how to respond," she whispered quietly.

"Oh Poppy, I'm not looking for any particular response." He brushed back the hair from her temple, loving how she leaned into his touch.

"Dex, can I be honest?"

"Always."

"Um." She licked her lips, all teasing gone, she looked nervous.

"Kenna, what is it?"

She took a deep breath. "Look, I'm just a dumbass okay? I should have just got right back on the horse, you know? Jaden was awful. I let him fuck with my head. I think I had offers." Her fingers trembled as she touched her neck. "No, I mean, of course, I had opportunities." She took another deep breath and pushed against him, struggling to get out of his lap.

He kept her in place. "You're not going anywhere."

"Let me up. What I have to say is stupid enough, without saying it while in some man's lap."

"First, you're not on *some man's* lap. You're in *my* arms. And sweetheart, let me see if I can make the second part easy. You're picky, and it's been a while, right?"

She stopped squirming and looked up at him.

"Oh, let's just call this out. I'm not picky, I'm neurotic. If I were a normal woman, I would have had a lover since Jaden. I haven't, okay? I'm coming up on my ten-year anniversary of celibacy. Do you really want to have a relationship with somebody that crazy?" This time when she pushed against him, her hand hit his crotch. She turned bright red.

"Seeing as how you just tested my level of interest, I think it's safe to assume I want a relationship." Dex smiled.

"Umm."

"But Sweetheart, it's more than that, okay? I want more than just sex. I want your time. Your smiles. Your neurosis. I want to really get to know your son. Your mom. I want to know what you like to order at an Italian restaurant. I want to know what your favorite movie is. What you wear to bed at night. I want to know why in the hell you would think that you're crazy when you've done nothing but protect yourself from being hurt again. But what I really want to know is if you will trust me with a little piece of your heart."

Her eyes welled up with tears. "Oh God, that's beautiful."

"No, you're beautiful."

She sucked in a deep breath.

"Will you come upstairs with me?" he asked.

She nodded.

He stood up with her still in his arms.

"You're going to carry me?" she whispered.

"I'm sure as hell not giving you a chance to get away."

Her soft laugh tinkled like bells. It also told him that she was with him.

Thank God!

Soon they were in the room that he had commandeered. Kenna was clutching his neck so tightly he thought he might lose circulation. When he looked into her sweet face, he could see panic laced with determination. That was his woman. No matter her fears, she would never back down, but that wasn't he wanted for them. For her.

Dex kicked the door closed with his foot, then went to the bed and sat down with her in his lap.

"Lasagna."

"Huh?" he queried.

"I always order lasagna. With meat sauce. I wear Navy T-shirts to bed with comfy shorts."

His head went quiet. The world stopped spinning. "Why do you wear Navy T-shirts to bed?"

"My dad was in the Navy. He wore dress whites when he married my mom. I wear Navy T-shirts to bed."

"Is that why you responded to my e-mail? The dress whites?"

"That, and you're a big brother to a boy who needs you and your eyes. You have beautiful eyes. I thought maybe you could be someone I could trust with a piece of my heart."

"Ahhh God, you kill me." He pressed a kiss against her temple, then feathered his lips down the line of her jaw until he could capture her lips. So good, she tasted so good. He laid her down on the duvet, strands of strawberry blonde hair fanned across the blue pillows. Her hazel eyes looked mostly gray as they stared up at him.

"What are you thinking?" he asked.

"I want this," she whispered.

"I'm glad." Her fingers went to the buttons on her blouse, he brushed them away. "I want to undress you. I've dreamt of taking it slow, savoring every moment."

Her voice was hushed. "Really?"

"Truly," he whispered the word against her lips. His fingers slowly slipped first one, then another and then another button from their holes until he was able to part her shirt and look at the sensible white bra that encased her generous breasts.

It broke his heart when he saw her waiting for his judgement like there was a possibility that he would find her lacking. "Lady, you take my breath away."

A smile, like the sun cresting the ocean at dawn, broke over her face. He dipped down for another kiss and was soon lost. The woman was as potent as Kentucky bourbon. He felt her hands under his T-shirt, her nails scraping up his back, and the caress was going to make this moment go a whole lot faster than he wanted.

"Off," she whispered.

"What?"

"Your shirt off. Now!" Her nails bit deep, and he liked it. He pulled it over his head and was gratified when he heard her sigh of satisfaction.

"Now you." He eased her up, so he could pull off her blouse and unfasten her bra. Thank God, he was lying down. Otherwise, she'd bring him to his knees.

"Fuck. You're gorgeous," he rasped.

She stilled. Her eyes got wide. Then she threw back her head and laughed.

* * *

"Woman, there better be a damn good reason you're laughing."

Kenna wound her arms around his neck and tried to pull him down for a kiss. He was having none of it. "You really think I'm beautiful," she said grinning.

"No. Get it right, I think you're beyond beautiful. I said you're gorgeous."

She laughed harder. "Now kiss me."

He looked put out. She grabbed his ears and pulled. His lips met her smile, and it was a glorious, beautiful, gorgeous kiss. It was the best kiss of her entire life. Each one of his kisses just kept getting better. She felt his hands move up her ribcage, up and up, then he was cupping her breasts. She closed her eyes even tighter so she could relish the sensation. Tendrils of heat coiled outwards, her legs started moving of their own volition. Her thighs squeezing together, trying to assuage the fire that Dex had started.

She didn't know when her hands had moved, but once again she felt the strength of Dex's strong back under fingers. She pressed deep into his flesh, savoring the resiliency of his muscles. Dex moved his mouth, she felt the rasp of his beard against her cheek, then he moved lower, and...

Gods, Yes!

His tongue circled her nipple. Hot, wet, sublime.

"Dex," she gasped. "I need...I need."

His eyes shot up and caught hers. "I have you. I'll take care of you. Always."

He bent back to taste her and she couldn't think, she could only feel. His flesh against hers, his arms beneath her back, she was wrapped up in the heat and scent of Dex, and she gloried in it.

Kiss after kiss, caress after caress, and then she found herself lying on the bed without her jeans, looking at him wearing just her panties. Her plain white cotton panties.

"No thong."

"These are now my favorite type of panties," he whispered.

His fingers traced the elastic of her waistband, back and forth, shooting tingles through her body. Then he slid his hand underneath the cotton, and she held her breath. His eyes met hers.

"Breathe Baby." One finger found her wet flesh, and she gasped for air.

His eyes glittered with passion and tenderness as he coaxed a response that had been waiting just for him. Just him. He pressed and swirled and she arched against the heat of his hand.

Was that her making those sounds?

Then all thought flew out of her head as her release exploded.

He got off the bed and stripped. Her eyes widened as she saw him naked for the first time, his body was a work of art. But she saw scars. Before she had a chance to fully comprehend what those meant, he had grabbed a condom from his duffel and whisked her panties off her body.

"Are you okay with this," he asked.

Where was her resounding 'yes?' She could only give a small nod. But he understood, his fingers trailed down her cheek.

"We'll go slow. Snail's pace slow." Then his fingers continued a path to her breasts.

"Fuck slow," she said finding her words. "I need you now."

He grinned. "There's my girl."

She pushed up on her elbows and parted her legs, anxious to start. He cocked an eyebrow, and cupped her breast, his thumb rasping against her nipple. She gasped. He bent down and sucked the other one, and she moaned. Soon he had her writhing on the bed. Thank God, his room was far from the others, was her last coherent thought as he slid down her body between her thighs.

He wasn't.

He couldn't.

His thumbs touched and caressed and parted her needy flesh. Then his tongue was there, and she cried out his name as she found rapture.

Soon she was locked in his arms, her face smashed against his chest. Her hand moved to his cock and found him sheathed.

"Please, Dex." She moved her leg so that it circled his waist.

"Slow, Baby," he admonished.

"Now," she said as she guided him to her. "Now, now, now."

He thrust deep. She winced.

"Goddammit, Kenna."

"I'm good." She clutched him with both legs when he would have pulled away. "It's been awhile," she reminded him.

He remained still, and she absorbed the fullness, the closeness, the intimacy. She kissed the underside of his jaw and surged against him.

She squeezed, then squeezed again. He groaned.

Gently he moved. It felt good.

"Again," she pleaded.

He did, he kept moving, and soon they were locked in a rhythm that took her breath away. It was perfect. Every time she needed something, he gave it to her. She stared up at him, hoping that she was providing even half as much in return.

"Hey, stay with me," he admonished.

How had he known?

She closed her eyes and then felt lonely, missing the connection. She opened them again.

"That's it, Kenna, look at me. I need you." She saw he wasn't lying. Their emotional link was as deep and powerful as the joining of their bodies. He smiled, and she saw his pleasure, his joy.

She undulated against him.

"Again. Oh God, Kenna, do that again."

She did. Their passion became frenzied. He was taking her even higher than before. How was that even possible? Then she understood. It was because they were together.

"Kenna?"

"I'm here. Please. Now," she cried out.

She looked into the eyes of the man she loved and catapulted into bliss.

CHAPTER TEN

Austin, Penny, and Kenna were safely ensconced behind the gated estate of Rosalie Randall. He wasn't going to allow them to go to Rosalie's place until she had offered a Cadillac Escalade with tinted windows to go back and forth through her secured gates and up to her mansion. The school was e-mailing Austin's assignments, and under protest, Kenna had agreed to take two days off from work. That left Dex with some leeway to sort out Warren and Sanchez.

"What the fuck were you thinking?" he demanded when he arrived at the precinct.

The two detectives had taken Dex into a small conference room. It was probably used for interrogations, he thought. Which was perfect.

"We were checking into the flowers, then tapping and tracing her phone. We were doing our jobs." Warren was pissed.

"Well, if you had called Clint Archer like I'd requested, you would have found out that he had already tapped and traced her goddamn phone so you wouldn't have had to do double work!"

"Mr. Evans—"

"I'm not done," Dex interrupted Warren. "For a solid day, you left my woman swinging in the wind. This guy knows things about her that only someone who has really studied her would know."

"We know this," Sanchez said patiently.

"It's the dating site," Dex started.

"We get that!" Warren bit out. "You *all* are part of that goddamn site. Just how many women have you contacted anyway?"

"If you'd made a fucking phone call to Clint he could have explained exactly what the fuck was going on. You'll also notice that my profile was pretty fucking recent, and I checked, Jean wasn't one of the women contacted. But that was just blind fucking luck."

"What do you mean by that?" Sanchez asked politely.

"Yeah, explain it to us," Warren growled.

"So, this good cop, bad cop, is a real thing?" Dex asked. He was getting sick of this.

"Clive, take it down a notch," Sanchez said to his partner. "No, this isn't a real thing. We're kicking our own asses for not calling your friend. There isn't an excuse. We fucked up. We were going to talk to Ms. Wright yesterday after we checked some things out. We wanted to make sure that you weren't a suspect. Explain to us what you mean it was just blind luck that you hadn't contacted Jean Baldwin."

Shit. Fuck. Piss. He was so going to kill Clint.

"It was a practical joke. Clint set up a profile for me on CaliSingles. Then he sent out an e-mail to I don't know how many women saying I was interested in them. The blind luck part was that Jean wasn't one of those women. Two hundred and twenty-eight of them responded. It took me three god-damn days to respond to them all."

"You actually responded to them?" Warren said, his disbelief plain.

"Well yeah." Dex rubbed the back of his neck.

"What did you tell them?" Sanchez asked.

"I told them my profile had been hacked."

Sanchez laughed. "That must have gone over well."

"You don't know the half of it."

"And Ms. Wright?" Sanchez prompted.

"She was the one woman I didn't blow off. She wrote the funniest damned response. I couldn't pass her up."

Warren leaned forward. "Did you tell her that it was a set-up?" he asked menacingly.

Great, she'd managed to find another protector.

"Yep, I fessed up on our first date. She rolled with it. Another reason that I'm keeping her."

Sanchez grinned. Warren looked disgruntled. Well, the man would just have to deal.

"Could you please get back to the point that Archer tapped her phone. Are you saying you have a recording of the call? Do you know where it originated?"

Dex pulled out his cell phone and prided himself on not slamming it down on the table. "You can listen to the call right now. Kenna did her best to keep him talking, but when you listen, you'll figure out he was planning on saying everything he did."

"He meant it to last as long as it did." Sanchez rolled his head.

"Listen for yourself." Dex played the recording. He was satisfied to see that both detectives let themselves show anger when Austin was threatened.

"Let me guess, when you traced the phone, it was a burner," Warren said disgustedly.

"You got it in one," Dex agreed. "Clint was on it when it came in. But the area he was able to triangulate it to was pretty fucking large. It was smack dab in the middle of the five, eight-oh-five and fifty-two freeways."

"That doesn't give us anything." Warren slammed his binder shut.

"You listened to the recording, you heard how short it was. Could you have done better?"

Warren opened his mouth, then shut it.

"No, we couldn't have done better," Sanchez admitted.

Dex's phone vibrated. Austin's name came up on the screen. "I need to take this."

The cops nodded.

"Yo," he answered.

"Dex? You need to get here now." The kid sounded wrong.

"What's going on? Are you all right? Is your mom okay?"

"Dex! Please man." He heard the kid swallow. He put his phone on speaker. "You gotta come to Rosalie's. I got an e-mail. I can't let Mom see it." Austin's voice stuttered. "Dex. He killed her."

Dex didn't think he heard him right, he was talking fast in the end.

"What did you say?"

"I didn't watch it all. It's a video. It came to me from school. He's hurting her. Bad. Get here!" The last was an order. "Mom can't see this."

Then he choked out again. "I don't know what to do...There was so much blood."

"I'll be there. Hold on, Son."

The phone went dead.

"What the fuck?" Warren said.

"They're holed up at Rosalie's." Dex's hand was on the conference room door. Sanchez and Warren were up and following behind him.

* * *

Austin was waiting for him outside on the front steps at the top of the circular drive. He was pacing back and forth. His eyes immediately took in the second car that pulled in behind Dex's jeep.

"Who are they?" he asked as Dex bounded up the stairs.

"They're cops. I was at the police station when you called."

"Mom will figure out something's up."

"Where is she?"

"She's in Rosalie's office."

Dex nodded. "Got it. We'll go around the back to the verandah. You go in and bring your laptop to us."

"I didn't think of that," Austin said.

For the first time since he'd met him, he seemed like the fifteen-year-old boy that he was. Dex cupped the back of his head. "It's understandable, Austin. You're doing great."

"It's bad," he whispered. Dex heard the tremor in the boy's voice.

"We'll get through it together," he assured him.

Austin nodded. "I'll meet you in five."

Then he was gone.

Dex turned around and faced the detectives. "Let's park around back with the other cars, so we're not so obvious. We're trying to fly under the radar for the time being."

"We'll follow you," Warren said.

Dex moved his jeep back behind the garages. When he got out, he motioned for the detectives to follow him.

When they got to the verandah, Austin was standing there holding his laptop in his hand. The four of them huddled up. "We can't look at it out here. You need to hear the sound, and anybody could come by." The kid had a point. Austin pointed across the yard to the greenhouse.

Dex looked at the house and calculated. The office was on the other side, looking out over the side lawn, not the back lawn. They should be good. They made their way over to the greenhouse. One gardener was in it. Dex asked him to give them some privacy. He looked at him confused. Then he and Sanchez repeated the request in Spanish at the same time. Sanchez grinned at him. Dex didn't give a shit that Sanchez was impressed he spoke Spanish, he was just happy the gardener left, and they could see what was on Austin's computer.

"Did you say you got this e-mail from school?" Warren asked.

"Yeah, I've been getting a lot of my homework from school. This had my school's address, so I opened it. I didn't recognize the teacher's name, but I figured it was just a substitute. There was a video attached. Sometimes it's like that."

He opened his laptop and clicked to his e-mail files. "Here it is. Mr. Forrester." Austin's finger trembled as he pressed the button to open the e-mail.

"Austin. You've already watched it. Why don't you go outside?" Dex said quietly.

"I should watch all of it. I can handle it."

"Austin, I don't doubt it. But this shit eats away at your soul. Life's going to scar you enough over the years. If you can hold out a little longer so that you can take more hits later...well...you're better off."

"Won't it help Mom, if I watch? Try to get in this bastard's head?" he asked grimly.

"If there is the slightest, the tiniest way you can be of service to get this fucker, I'll call you back in. You have my word."

Hazel eyes might have shown relief, but there was also resolve. He was his mother's son.

"I'll be on the lookout for Mom or anyone else."

"Good man."

He watched the door close behind Austin, then he went back to Warren, Sanchez and the computer. Sanchez had the video queued up.

A man was wearing a black leather mask that was found in sex stores. His eyes and mouth were cut out. His face filled the screen.

"Hello Austin," he said with the same raspy voice they'd just heard in the police station. "It's time for a biology lesson. Or shall we call it psychology and anatomy?"

He stepped back from the camera. He was dressed in a billowy black shirt so it was hard to determine his shape. A woman was tied to a ladderback chair. She was wearing a hospital gown. It was torn open; her left breast was exposed. There was blood covering the white garment, it was clear that it had dripped down from slices across her face, neck, and breast. Before Dex had a chance to brace, a whip whistled through the air and sliced through her gown. Blood danced upwards from her chest as she screamed. He took the end of the whip between his hands and walked back to the camera. As soon as his face filled the screen, he licked the blood off the leather.

"I'm doing this because I couldn't find your mother, Austin. All I wanted to do was see her. I wouldn't hurt her. I just like looking at her. But because she wasn't at your house or the hospital, I had to do this." He took another lick.

"She tastes so good." He turned and raised the whip again. Hitting her body, her face. More shrieks. More blood. Then Dex watched stone faced as the monster raised the bullwhip and swung it sideways, wrapping it around her neck. Then he yanked hard.

"Mom, no!" Dex glanced over his shoulder. He could see shadows through the green glass door, but it didn't open. Austin must have held Kenna back.

Dex turned his attention back to the screen. Horror and relief slid through him as he realized the man had broken the woman's neck.

Casually the monster walked back to the camera.

"Austin, it's your mother's fault. It's her fault. I just wanted to see her walking into your house last night. I like watching her walk. But she denied me even that small pleasure. What other choice did I have? I hope you were educated."

He laughed. He picked the camera up off the stand and walked it to the body of the woman, scanning in on her feet, her legs, up and up until it reached her face.

"No. I don't think they'll be able to identify her. Pity."

The camera blinked off.

"Motherfucker!" Warren yelled.

The door to the greenhouse smashed open. "What is going on?" Kenna raged.

"Mom, it's okay."

"Don't 'it's okay' me. I want to know what the fuck is going on." Her hands were on her hips. She looked enraged, but Dex could see fear below the anger.

"It's not something you need to see," Sanchez said when her eyes lighted on the computer.

"Don't piss on me and tell me it's raining," she stormed.

"He's killed another one," Warren said.

Dex whirled on the man at the same time that Kenna said, "What?!"

"The killer, he sent Austin a video of his latest kill," Warren said grimly.

"Get the fuck out of here. Now." Dex was ready to tear Clive Warren apart, and as soon as he said those words, it was like the man came out of a trance.

"Jesus, I'm sorry Kenna, I mean Ms. Wright, I shouldn't have said it like that. It's just that video. It took me by surprise."

"My son saw a video of someone getting murdered?" Kenna all but shrieked.

Austin looked gut shot. It was exactly what he hadn't wanted to happen.

"Austin, I've got this," Dex said. Austin gave him a long look, then went to his mom and hugged her.

"Sweetheart, talk to me," she said.

"I will soon," he promised her.

"Go with him," Dex said to the two cops.

"I'm so sorry," Warren began.

"Out!" Dex roared. Sanchez grabbed his partner's arm, and they followed Austin out of the greenhouse.

"Dex, talk to me."

He pulled her gently into his arms. She struggled. "Let me see what's on the computer."

"No."

"Yes. If Austin saw it, then I need to see it."

"No, you don't." He pulled her head down to his chest.

She clutched him close, then peered up at him. "It's that bad? My baby saw somebody being killed? How bad was it?"

"He said he didn't watch it all."

"Are you sure he didn't?"

"Yes, Kenna, I'm sure."

She shoved her face into his shirt. Her shoulders began to shake, but she didn't make a sound. He stroked his hands down her back.

"Let it out."

"I can't. I need to talk to Austin."

"Let it out. Rant. Cry. Scream. Beat on me. Do whatever you need to do, Baby. I'm here for you."

"I need to keep it together. I need to go talk to my son."

He understood. He admired. "But after you're done, you'll come back to me?"

She pushed out of his arms to look up at him. He saw steely determination in her gold-flecked hazel eyes. "I'll come back to you, but not for fucking comfort. We're going to talk about you going behind my back about something concerning my child."

The corner of his mouth kicked up. God, she was gorgeous when she went mama bear.

"Don't you fucking smile at me. I'm pissed."

"And that's why I'm smiling."

"If you say I'm beautiful when I'm angry, I'll kick you in the balls."

Dex had to bite his tongue from laughing. She was beautiful when she was angry. "Go talk to your son. I'll be waiting for you on the verandah."

* * *

Kenna tapped on Austin's door.

"Come in, Mom."

He was sitting on the bed in the room that Rosalie had provided for him, his head bent, his hands clasped in front of him. She pulled over the rolling desk chair, so she was seated in front of him. She covered his hands with hers, and he immediately turned his over and grabbed hers. When had his hands gotten so big?

She looked at the top of his head for long moments, and then finally he looked up. His hazel eyes were swimming with tears.

"Mom," he said hoarsely. His hands clenched hers tighter, and she hid her wince of pain.

"Tell me, Baby."

He straightened, then cleared his throat. He blinked rapidly, and the tears were gone. "We need to keep you safe."

"We are Honey," she said firmly.

"We need to leave the state. Go someplace else. He knows Rosalie's house. He knows our house. He knows...he knows..." his voice trailed off.

"The police will keep me safe. They're tracking him right now. I'm sure this new video will offer clues."

"It's not good enough. You don't know. I don't want you to know." He turned back to her, his face once again filled with anguish.

"Dex said you didn't watch the whole thing. Did you?"

"No. He said I'd end up with enough scars on my soul eventually, and I didn't need this one." Austin quietly repeated Dex's beautiful advice.

"He's right."

"But if it would have helped, we both agreed I would watch. And I would have."

Her heart ached with pride for this man child in front of her. "I know you would have. I thank God you didn't need to, but I know you would have." She pulled up his clenched hands and kissed them.

"Can we leave, Mom?"

"I'm not sure that will work. If it will keep you safe. We're out of here. But first, you have to answer a question for me."

He looked up at her questioningly.

"Why did you call Dex? Why not come to me?"

His answer was swift and sure. "I knew he wouldn't let you see it. I knew he would protect you from it, and take care of things."

Fuck.

How did she say this? "I know Dex has inserted himself in our lives. But, Honey, he's just a man I'm dating. He's not my protector."

Austin's lips ticked upward, and he snorted. "Then you're not paying attention."

She dropped his hands and reared backwards. "I beg your pardon?"

"He's got it bad for you."

"Austin, I know this is the first time you've ever seen me in a relationship, but you've got it wrong. Dex and I are in the get to know one another stage. I don't know where we're going to end up. I don't want you to think this could end up permanent."

Austin gave her a pitying look. "Believe what you need to believe. As a matter of fact, I don't know why I even brought up the idea of us leaving. Your future is here. This fucker will be caught."

She just stared at her child, wondering when she had lost control.

CHAPTER ELEVEN

It had been four days since the video had been sent to Austin. He'd talked a reluctant Kenna into requesting the entire week off. All of Austin's homework assignments were now being sent to Clint Archer's e-mail, then scrubbed and forwarded to Dex, scrubbed again then they came to Austin. Penny was more than happy catching up on her backlist of books on her kindle. That meant that two people in the Wright household were kept busy.

Dex was finding out a lot about Kenna's personality, and number one was that she hated being idle. Jack and Beth's house was neat as a pin, but it now looked brand new. Every nook and cranny sparkled. Kenna had even taken out every item from the cupboards and washed them, then she washed the interiors of the cabinets and put down new contact paper.

"Seriously, Kenna, you need to stop," Dex admonished. "Beth is going to get a complex when she gets home. She's going to think you thought she wasn't clean."

Kenna's eyes got wide. "Oh my God, I'd never thought of that. What am I going to do? I threw away the old contact paper."

Dex gave a tired laugh. This was not a good situation. They were all on pins and needles. Eventually, Kenna's vacation would run out. He wasn't worried about his time off because he had a plan...that he needed to talk to her about.

"Poppy, can you sit down for a moment?"

"I know that look. It's not good. Has something happened? Has there been another murder?"

He cuddled her closer on the sofa. "Shit, I'm sorry. I'm going about this wrong. No, it's nothing like that. I have to go to the base tomorrow. Hunter is coming over to help you with household chores. What do you have on the agenda, cleaning the crown molding?"

"Hunter? Why do we need anyone? Nobody knows where we are. That doesn't make any sense."

He pulled her closer, for a quick kiss. "Humor me."

"No, seriously. I want to understand this. We're safe here. Why should I need a Navy SEAL babysitting me when I wash the windows?"

He sat up straight. "This is a two-story house. You're not planning on washing the windows, are you?"

"I was until you said that about Beth. Now stay on point, why do I need Hunter here if we're safe? I thought you said we're safe." Her voice trembled just the slightest bit.

His hand caressed her bare arm, she had goosebumps, and he hated knowing they were from fear. "Poppy, you need to humor me. The world I live in, shit happens. So, I take precautions with what is mine. As a matter of fact, we need to talk about where we're going next."

"Jack and Beth are coming home next week," she said softly. "I want to thank them for letting us have this place. If things were normal, I'd go and buy flowers and have champagne waiting for them in the fridge." Her expression changed from frightened to pissed. "I am so sick of not being able to do one darn thing that is normal. You do realize you bought the wrong kind of tomato sauce for the meatloaf, don't you? You won't even let me go to the grocery store. I can't depend on Hunter to pick up the right flowers for Beth," her breath caught at the end.

"Baby—"

"No Dex, I can't take it anymore." She pushed up off the couch and marched into the kitchen.

"What are you doing?"

"I'm not upset anymore, I'm mad." She grabbed her purse and pulled out the new cell phone that he had purchased for her from the electronics store. She punched one of the keys.

"Detective Warren? This is Kenna Wright. Have you caught him yet?" Uh-oh, the poor guy better watch out.

"Put it on speaker, Baby," Dex requested. She shook her head.

She listened to whatever Warren was saying.

"Well, have you found her body? Do you know who she is?"

She listened some more, her expression getting darker.

"For God's sake, there was a video. Do I need to look at it and figure this out for you?" Her tone could strip paint.

She listened.

"What messages has he left on my cell phone? I want to hear them!"

Dex had enough of this shit. He held out his hand and matched her glare for glare. She didn't hand him the phone, she put the phone on the counter and pressed the speaker button. Warren was talking.

"...point in you listening. It will just upset you."

"Clive, this is Dex. Kenna put it on speaker."

"Tell her she doesn't want to hear those messages. You know they'll just freak her out," the detective said.

Kenna whirled. "You've heard them?! Goddammit, Dex! If you've heard them, why haven't I? Just because you two have penises does not mean that you all are in charge. Dex is not the police so why in the hell has he heard these messages, and I haven't, Clive?" She packed a great deal of derision in that last word.

"Kenna, calm down," Dex said. "Clive here did not betray doctor patient privilege or whatever shit you want to call this. Clint is still listening into your calls."

"I want to hear those tapes now." She folded her arms over her chest.

"No," Dex said immediately. "It serves no purpose."

"I will not be a mushroom."

Dex chuckled.

"What?" Clive asked.

"Kept in the dark and fed bullshit."

"Oh." Dex could tell that Warren didn't know how to respond.

"Honest to God, what purpose would it serve?" Dex asked reasonably.

"I'd know what was going on. I need to know what's going on! Don't you understand?"

"He's one of the men who pinged you on the dating site," Dex answered. "I'm going through them every night. Clint and I both are. We're eliminating as we go."

"Wait just a damned minute, we're taking care of this. Our techs are damn good," Warren said. Dex could tell the man was pissed.

"We've seen their efforts. They're missing things."

There was a long pause. "You've hacked into our system?"

Now Dex was pissed. He leaned over the phone and said softly, "I asked to work with you. I asked nicely three different fucking times."

"This is police business. You're a Navy guy, go do Navy things."

Kenna put her hand on Dex's arm. It was nice, but it sure as hell wasn't going to help the detective.

"Clive. I think we're done here," Dex said.

"Well did you and your friend find this out? We just got this information confirmed this morning. There are two missing women in the last two weeks who somewhat match who we saw in that video. One of whom was on the dating site. Betchya didn't know that, now did you, big guy?"

He didn't. It pissed him off.

"Did you know that there are five profiles using the same IP address? They all contacted Jean and Kenna. Did you know that this IP address was bounced to hell and back, but we finally found out it originated at a Starbucks in La Jolla?" Dex asked.

There was a long pause, then Warren sighed. "You win, we'll share. I've got more. We've done a cross-check on our missing person database. Three months ago, there was another woman who went missing. She was on the CaliSingles dating site. Goddammit, we had a serial killer all along, and didn't know it," Warren said disgustedly.

"Why not?" Kenna asked.

"Her ex-husband had put her into the hospital twice. The detectives working the case have focused entirely on him, they never even noted that she was on the CaliSingles dating site in her case file. When we talked to them, they said they hadn't scrubbed her files off her computer. Total negligence."

"Are there any others? How far back have you looked? CaliSingles has been in operation for three years." Dex looked over at Kenna she was pale and shivering. He put his arm around her.

"We're pulling all of our missing women for the last three years and checking CaliSingles. Now tell me about the IP address. You think that our guy used five different profile names?" Warren asked.

"Yes. Clint is already putting together the time stamps so you can try to pick up any video they might have from the coffee shop. As a matter of fact, you should already have it in your e-mail," Dex said dryly.

There was a pause. "You mean you were going to share this all along?"

Dex got pissed. "I was going to share this. This isn't a goddamn pissing match. This is Kenna's life for fuck's sake."

"Yeah, yeah. What was I thinking?"

Kenna jerked out of his arms. "Now with all of this information, can you get him?" she asked Warren.

"It's a good start."

"What do you mean start?" she cried. "The first woman was killed three months ago. Jean's been dead for over three weeks. He just murdered someone on camera four days ago. How can you say you're just starting?"

"Dammit, Kenna, you're twisting it around. I just meant we're in better shape at this moment than we were a half hour ago."

"What did those text messages say? It's because he can't get to me, isn't it?"

Fuck, how had she put that together, Dex wondered.

"Yes, he's escalated since you've disappeared," Warren confirmed.

"We don't know that." Dex glared at the phone. "Baby, he's a psycho, he gets off on killing, he was doing it three months ago, way before you disappeared, way before you stopped taking his calls."

"Dex," she said softly, carefully. "When did the first e-mail come to me from this guy?"

Damn, he didn't want to tell her. She stared him down.

"Ten months ago, you got the first one from one of his profiles."

"And?" she asked.

"He kept pinging you, but they really started coming in hot and heavy from every profile four months ago."

"So right before the first murder."

He nodded. He saw her beautiful eyes fill with tears.

"And Jean? Jean was murdered after I took my profile down."

Fuck, she put that together too. He didn't want too, but he nodded.

Tears slipped down her face.

"Warren, we're done." He pressed end on the phone. Warren was saying something, but he didn't care. Kenna was what mattered.

He tugged her into his arms. "Baby, don't do this. This isn't your fault."

"I should have been paying attention. I should have done what you did. If I had responded and said I wasn't interested, then he wouldn't have gotten upset."

They were on the first floor of the house, Penny was in the living room, and Austin was in the den playing video games. He grabbed Kenna's hand. "Come with me, Baby. We need to talk in private."

"Oh God, Austin could have come in during this conversation."

"He didn't. It's all good."

He drew her out of the kitchen. When they walked past Penny in the living room, she looked up from her Kindle. She looked at her daughter, and then at Dex.

"You got this?" she asked him.

"Yes."

It said a whole hell of a lot about Kenna's state of mind that she didn't tear into either of them. She just docilely followed Dex up the stairs.

* * *

"You make your bed," Kenna noted absently as she swiped at her eyes.

"Sit down." He positioned her on the bed, then crouched in front of her.

She looked into his worried brown eyes. "I'm all right. Really, I am. I won't clean even." She looked past him to the window. If she didn't clean, and she didn't go to work, what was she going to do?

"Kenna—"

"Nope. I'm fine. Nothing to worry about." She looked past him to the window. There was bird shit on the screen. It needed cleaning. She turned back to Dex, "I just don't get it, ya know? I didn't do anything different than a lot of other women. I thought it was okay. Did I really do something that bad?"

"Baby, no."

"But I must have. I should never have set up a profile, and if I did, I should have..." Her shoulders slumped. She didn't know what. It was beyond her. An image of Jean in green corduroy jeans and a gold sweater, having a beer in her backyard. She'd been laughing.

"Baby, you need to stop crying."

What was he saying?

Another time, Jean had been at the hospital crying because a young father had died from injuries sustained in a car wreck. Kenna preferred the laughing Jean, but she'd probably been crying when she died...or screaming.

"Do you think she screamed? Did he make Jean scream?" she asked Dex.

"Don't do this to yourself," he said hoarsely.

"You're right, he didn't make her scream, *I* made her scream. It was because of me." Pretty, laughing Jean. She got her killed. Murdered. Tortured. All because she hadn't been nice to a man. It made no sense, it hurt her heart, it hurt her head. She gasped out a wrenching sob.

"I have you." And he did. She fell forward into Dex's arms.

She clutched his shoulders and let a river of pain drown his shirt, his neck. He said nonsense things. Things that she couldn't hear or comprehend, but they made her feel better. He finally eased her back up on the bed. She hiccupped.

"Wait here." He got up and got her a mound of tissue. She sobbed and mopped and blew and then was able to breathe in a steady breath.

Dex rested his hands on her thighs. "Feeling better?"

"Yeah."

"Can I talk you out of believing this isn't your fault?"

She shook her head; her hair went flying. He tamed it back and cupped her cheeks. His brown eyes were intense.

"Okay, then I need you to talk yourself out of believing it wasn't your fault. Close your eyes."

She looked at him confused.

"Baby, just do it. Close your eyes. Trust me."

Slowly she did. Jean smiled gently at her, then was gone. Her eyes shot open.

"Close them, Baby. I want to do an exercise."

"Okay," she said slowly. In her mind, she said good-bye to Jean, then closed her eyes.

"Hold Austin's hands, can you do that? He's crying." Kenna cringed. But she pictured it. "Ten years from now the exact thing that is happening in your life is happening in his. He decided to meet someone and join a dating site. Other men are getting killed by some unknown female, and he knows he's to blame. He *knows* it Kenna, and he's inconsolable."

She opened her eyes.

His hand brushed over her lids. "Keep them closed," he whispered gently. "He's a target, Kenna. Austin is a target of this madwoman, but he thinks it's his fault. He thinks the men who died should hate him. And Austin is a victim. Can you help him let it go? Can you help him past that bullshit in his head?"

She tilted her head upwards and opened her eyes, avoiding Dex's gaze.

Dex was right. It would kill her if Austin were taking on that burden. Was she really going to go through the bullshit of thinking this was her fault? Really? Could she be responsible for some maniac? She tilted her head back down to Dex.

"Yep, I'm done. This isn't my fault."

"Just like that, huh?"

"Just like that," she concurred. His eyes were sparkling. "Because you're just that good Mr. Evans. Goddamn, fucking, dammit, this is not my fault!"

"Nope."

She threw her arms around his neck and took a deep breath. "Okay, okay, okay. I'm putting that thinking to bed. It serves no purpose."

She felt Dex's shoulders shake.

"Are you laughing?" she demanded. He couldn't possibly be laughing at a time like this.

"Damn right, I'm laughing. You fucking amaze me. I'm so proud of you."

"Oh." She sniffed. "Well, okay then."

She sat back on the bed and looked into his dancing brown eyes. Well, she might amaze him, but still.

"About me being amazing. You like it when I'm a straight shooter, right?"

"Absolutely."

"Good. Since you've brought up Austin, now I need to. I've got a problem. I need your help."

"I'll do whatever I can, you know that."

Could he be any more wonderful? She took a deep breath. "Austin has gotten it into his head that I'm someone special to you. Can you please set him straight?"

"Huh?" Dex looked totally confused.

"I know, right? Can you explain how things really are? Tell him that we're just... I don't know what, but that it's not a big relationship thing?"

Dex's eyes got dark. "What the hell are you talking about, Poppy?"

"Don't call me that." She twisted, trying to get off the bed. He pushed down on her thighs, keeping her in place.

"Okay, Kenna, then. Explain to me what you mean that we aren't in a big relationship thing because it sure feels like a big deal to me."

She was talking before he even finished. "Look Dex. I know you're doing the Navy SEAL protector thing, men like you can't help it. You're honorable. I get that. But you haven't exactly been chomping at the bit to get back in my bed."

"Haven't been chomping at the bit?" He shook his head. Slowly he stood up from his crouch and planted his hands on either side of her. She had to lean back to look in his face. His smile was blatantly sexy and amused. "You've really got yourself tied up in one interesting knot Poppy."

"Don't call me that!" She shoved at his shoulders, but he didn't move an inch.

"Kenna, you were a trembling mass of nerves after that video was sent. Then you went on a cleaning spree. I thought you wanted space." His eyes softened.

"I thought." She bit her lip. She was never in a million years going to tell him what she thought.

"What? What did you think?" he asked softly, kindly.

Fuck, she'd gotten it all wrong.

Time to save face.

"Just kiss me."

"Poppy, you can trust me. Tell me what you thought."

She smiled brightly, hoping to change the subject. "It's nothing, just old tapes."

In a maneuver she couldn't begin to comprehend, he was sitting on the bed, and she was in his lap. "It's that fucker of an ex-husband, isn't it. Don't listen to him. Get him out of your head." He pushed back her hair, his mouth hovered over hers. She could taste the mint of his breath. "You absolutely do it for me. Everything about you does it for me. Your smile, your eyes, the fire you constantly spit at me. Kenna Leigh, we have your son and your mom as chaperones, I've been trying to respect that. But fuck that shit."

He went in for the kill. His mouth didn't slam, didn't plunder, he feathered a kiss so sweet, so tender, she melted.

Tears pricked the back of her eyes as she wrapped her arms around his neck. Even the night they spent together couldn't match the love she felt pouring from him. That couldn't be right.

He lifted his head. "Are you getting it?"

"Huh?"

"I love you. I pray to God that you love me a little bit back."

Was he for real?

"Kenna, are you going to leave me hanging?"

She hit his shoulder. "Oh for God's sake. You know I'm in love with you," she spit out.

He burst out laughing. "I had an idea."

"Why didn't you tell me sooner?" she demanded.

"I thought *you* had an idea," he teased. "I didn't know you got twisted in your head." He brushed a kiss on the corner of her mouth. "But seriously, I thought that with everything that had gone on with the video and moving in here you didn't need to be pushed. I'm sorry, Baby."

"Dammit, Dex, if I'd wanted space, I would have said so. Don't just change on me. It freaks me out. I don't know to react. Don't do it again," she groused.

Her scowl turned into a glare when she saw him bite the inside of his lip. "Are you laughing?"

"Nope," he said with a laugh.

"Dammit!"

He tumbled her back onto the bed. His hands were underneath her sweater, and she began to writhe as he touched her waist, her ribs, her breasts.

"Is the door locked?" she asked breathlessly.

"Yep." He peeled the soft cotton over her head and stared at the swell of her breasts. Need suffused her body. She loved the heated look in his eyes. He made her feel beautiful.

"Shirt. Off."

"Demanding wench."

For a just a moment she worried, then she saw his approval, and she grinned. "Yes, I am. Now take off that shirt, I want to see you."

"Yes, ma'am."

* * *

He'd seen that flicker of worry, and he was determined that he was going to squelch it. Maybe not today, maybe not tomorrow. But soon this woman he loved would know that she was perfect the way she was. She'd know that there wasn't a move she could make that was wrong to his way of thinking.

He pulled off his shirt. He loved the desire shining in her eyes. Her hand fluttered upward, not quite touching. He grabbed it and placed it over his heart. "I want your hands all over me," he assured her.

"Honey, that wasn't reluctance. That was me trying to figure out where to start. You're a banquet for the senses. I was overwhelmed."

"God, do I understand that," he said in a hoarse voice. "You're exquisite."

Hands greedily slid over each other's bodies, and he soon had her naked.

"Not fair," she breathed. "Why do you still have your jeans on?"

"Because it'll be over too fast."

"I want fast. I need hard, fast and wild."

Dex shuddered at the pictures her words painted in his head. "No, Baby, we're going for slow strokes and sweet, tender lovemaking."

"I'm still voting for hard," she said as she cupped his cock through his jeans.

He burst out laughing. "Yes, I think I can guarantee you'll still be getting hard."

She arched up and gave him a hot, lush and wet kiss that made his head spin. His hand swept downwards, loving the warm, lavish contours of her body. He pushed apart her thighs needing the very heart of her. He touched her.

"You're perfect. So ready for me."

He tested her depths, and she arched against his fingers, gasping.

Dex gritted his teeth. Could he go slow? He was damned well going to try. His lips skimmed across her breast, and then his tongue softly caressed her nipple.

"No," she breathed out.

His head raised up to look at her.

"What, Baby?"

"I don't need tender and slow."

There had never been anyone who needed and deserved slow and tender more, not that he was going to tell her that. Show her, definitely. Tell her, not a chance in hell.

"*I* need it," he said. He rubbed the bristles of his beard against her tummy, and she mewled with pleasure. She clutched his hair. So damned responsive, she made him feel like a god. Touching, seeing and hearing her responses aroused him, but it was knowing that they had a heart connection that kicked him in the gut.

He stroked her thighs further apart, intent on pleasuring her even more. She pulled his hair. Hard. He lifted his head to look at blazing green, gray eyes.

"No! I want to taste you this time."

He grinned.

"We'll get there."

"Now!"

He pulled her fists out of his hair, thankful he kept it military short. Keeping hold of her wrists with one hand, he grabbed her ass with his other, then dipped down and licked.

"Dex," she panted. "You don't fight fair."

No, he didn't. He savored and teased. She trembled. He brought his fingers into play and smiled against her flesh as she gasped and called his name. Then he felt those first flutters that turned to convulsions. Her warmth cascaded down, and he reveled in it.

Before she had a chance to catch her breath, he stripped off his jeans and grabbed a condom. Her eyes drifted open. "Hey, it was my turn to taste," she protested.

"Tonight," he said softly as he nuzzled her neck.

"Promise?" Her hands were guiding him inwards.

"I'd promise you anything if you keep doing what you're doing."

Her long legs wrapped around him, her heels digging into his ass.

"Harder."

"I told you how it was going to be." He smiled down at her as he pushed in slowly. She clasped him close, and it was heaven. Watching her smile was almost as good as the feel of her tight heat. *Almost.*

He surged high and gave an internal roar of satisfaction when she moaned deeply. Oh yeah, he'd found the right spot. Again, and again he made sure he stroked that hidden point. And then he grinned with joy as he had to hold her tightly when she came apart in his arms, and he followed her. Nothing, absolutely nothing, had ever been better than making love with Kenna Leigh.

CHAPTER TWELVE

Kenna now knew that Hunter Diaz liked peanut butter cookies. Wyatt Leeds was a madman when it came to Grand Theft Auto. Dalton Sullivan had read almost all of the books she had, and he even admitted to liking one of her favorite romance authors. Griffin Porter had the cutest baby girl she had ever seen pictures of, and he loved his wife beyond reason. But this morning she had a problem that she needed to discuss with Dex before he left.

She knocked on his bedroom door. She did not sleep in Dex's room at night. She would go to him after she thought that Austin was asleep, they would make long glorious love, then she would go back to her room to sleep. Her son could probably handle it if she said she and Dex were lovers, but she didn't think she could handle having such a conversation. She would probably have a heart attack.

"Yo! Come in."

She went in. He was pulling on his shirt. Thank God it was her, thinking of heart attacks, her mother would have had one on the spot if she'd seen him shirtless. Of course, she would have died with a smile.

Dex came over and pulled her into his arms and kissed her.

"Good morning." He smiled.

"Morning." She bit her lip.

"Uh-oh. What's up."

"It's Austin. Okay, it's me too. It's Mom. It's all of us. Get us the hell out of here. We need out. But Austin's the worst. He's snapping, and grousing, and complaining about things that he would never complain about. Never in a million years. He complained about the macaroni and cheese. He said it was too cheesy, for God's sake."

Dex laughed.

She grabbed his cheeks. "This is not a laughing matter."

"Kids complain."

"I'm asking too much of *my* kid. He knows why we're holed up here. He knows there's somebody out to get me, and he's feeling emasculated about the whole deal. He can't see his friends, he can't go to school, and he's letting down the wrestling team. His words, not mine. I feel like I'm going to explode because I've been cooped up here, it's got to be ten times worse on him."

Dex pulled her hands away and kissed the insides of her wrists. "You're absolutely right, Kenna. I should have thought of that."

"No, you shouldn't have, it's not your place. I'm his mother."

Dex searched her face. "I *should* have thought of that. Are you getting me?"

"Um, no."

Dex sighed. "Kenna, I want to be allowed to think of that. I want to be allowed...by you...to worry about your son."

Shit, she hated the emotional baggage she carried around.

"Dex, you're going to have to spell this out for me."

"Kenna, before we can move forward in this relationship. I have to know if you trust me with your son. This can't work unless you will allow me to partner with you in his care and well-being."

Her legs trembled. He caught her around the waist. "We matter that much to you?"

"Yes. Yes, you do." His brown eyes were solemn.

She thought her face might split in half she was grinning so wide. She threw her arms around his neck. "Oh my God. Oh my God. Oh my God. You matter the world to me too."

He twirled her around. Even when he set her back down on the ground, it didn't feel like it, she thought she was walking on a cloud. This couldn't be happening to her. He cupped her face. "I love you, Poppy."

"I love you too, Dexter Anthony Evans."

The world faded away as they kissed.

The world came crashing back as she heard her name being called, "Mom!"

"She's in here," Dex called out.

Kenna looked at him in horror. He chuckled.

Dex's door opened. "Oh, there you are," Austin said. "Who is today's babysitter?" he asked Dex.

"Let's see if we can arrange Wyatt again, and maybe you guys can hit the waves. What do you think?"

Austin turned to Kenna. "For real?"

"If Dex says yes, then it's for real," she answered.

Austin's eyes lit up, and he let out a *Whoop*.

"Quiet, you'll wake up your grandmother," Kenna admonished.

"Let me give Wyatt a call. He should be able to trade his day off with Aiden." Dex went to grab his cell phone.

Austin came over and put his arm around her neck. "So, do you think it's time you quit sneaking around the halls in the middle of the night, or what?"

Kenna felt the blush starting at her toes and quickly rising to her scalp. Austin laughed.

"Seriously, Mom, this is cool."

"Okay, it's done. Austin, Wyatt's going to call you on that new cell phone you have. He has a wet suit that he says will fit you. He'll get you outfitted."

"This is great, we'll finally get the hell out of the house," Kenna said enthusiastically. "I can't wait to tell Mom." She turned to leave, and Dex grasped her hand.

"What?" she asked.

"If you're going too, we need to arrange a couple of more people."

Her shoulders sagged. "It's okay, I don't need to go."

He kissed her forehead. "Yes, you do. You need out of the house as much as Austin."

"She sure does. She's been getting pretty testy. Did you know that she complained that the macaroni and cheese didn't have enough cheese in it last night? Grandma was pissed."

Dex laughed. "I think all three of you need out of the house, like yesterday."

* * *

"Is it going to be a big deal that I really don't have much experience swimming in the ocean?" Austin asked. "I was on the swim team for three years in grade school."

"That'll help a lot," Wyatt said. "This is about being smart and listening to what I say. The swells are easy today here at Moonlight, I checked before coming, so that's why we're here. I just want to get you up on your knees on the board. That'll be a win."

"Just on my knees?"

"Dude, it'd be a miracle if you can make it on your feet today."

Holy shit, did Wyatt know what he was doing by daring her boy? Austin looked out at the waves with determination, and Wyatt looked at *her* and winked. Well, apparently, he did know what he was doing.

"You got my stuff? Remember Denny might call or text."

"I remember. I have your phone," she said with just a hint of exasperation. But mostly she was excited for her son. It was too bad her mom had a headache, she would have gotten a kick out of this.

Kenna sat with Hunter Diaz on top of one of the picnic tables so she could have a good view of the swelling surf of Moonlight Beach. There were plenty of surfers, young and old, in the water. There was also a concession stand that was closed and three volleyball courts, one that had a lively game going on.

Hunter pulled out a ball cap from his duffel. "Put this on."

"I put on sunscreen," she said.

"You need more than just sunscreen, you're awfully fair, and we're going to be here awhile." He leaned back on his elbows, and she watched him as he watched everything.

"Do all of you guys do that?"

"Do what?"

"Observe. Take in your whole environment. I've seen Dex do the same thing."

"It's our training."

She thought about it. "It's a chicken and an egg kind of thing. Do you think that you were kind of like that before hand, and that's the reason you took to the training?"

Hunter burst out laughing. God, he was gorgeous when he laughed.

"You've met Wyatt, haven't you?" he asked.

"'Nuff said." Wyatt was not the quiet and observant type, he ran on all cylinders at breakneck speed. "Some of the training must have been nails on the chalkboard for that poor kid," Kenna said.

"It sure as hell wasn't his nature," Hunter agreed.

Kenna shifted on the picnic table so she would be more comfortable.

"Look, Hunter!" She pointed. "Austin is on his knees!" It had been over an hour, she had seen him in the water more often than on the surfboard, but there he was balancing on his knees.

"He's going to get his legs under him in no time."

"Do you think?" she asked excitedly.

"Definitely." She rummaged through the backpack she'd brought, and then realized she'd left the peanut butter cookies in the truck. Dammit.

"Do you want a water?" she asked Hunter.

"Thanks," he said as he took a bottle. Austin's phone beeped with an incoming text. "That must be Denny. Hopefully, his mom can come by. Austin hasn't seen him since all of this shit started." She dug through Austin's backpack. God, the kid didn't keep anything organized. She found the phone at the bottom and pressed the display as she pulled it out of the sack. It was a text message, but not from Denny, she opened it.

Mary Poppins, if you talk to your bodyguard, Austin dies.

She looked at Hunter who was drinking his water and watching the surf, then she swiped her thumb over the attachment in the text and a picture of Austin came up. He was on the surfboard. In the middle of a rifle's cross-hairs.

Hunter looked over at her. "Everything all right? Is Denny coming?"

"Yep," she said brightly. "I have to text him back." Her thumbs were flying.

What do you want?

She waited for the answer.

There's an empty green Monte Carlo with a white top behind the concession stand. Get in it. Answer the phone in the car when it rings.

She sat there, unable to move. Unable to think.

"Kenna, are you all right?"

She nodded.

"What did Denny say?"

The phone beeped.

Get rid of the SEAL and go.

Hunter sat up. He was looking at her suspiciously. Oh God. She had to get it together. The phone beeped.

"Is that Denny?"

"Yes," she said quickly. Her palms were slick with sweat. "He's in the car with his mom. They'll be here any minute. I need to go to the truck and get the peanut butter cookies I made for you." She started to get up.

He put his hand on her arm. "I'll get them."

"No, I will." She was loud and harsh.

"Kenna, what's wrong?"

She took a deep breath and thought fast. "I think you were right, the sun is getting to me. I'm getting kind of a headache. I'm probably dehydrated." She took out a bottle of water for herself and took a swallow. "I'll go get the cookies."

"I'd prefer it if you'd stay where you are, especially if you're not feeling well." He smiled at her. "I'll go to the truck. Just sit back, watch Austin and Wyatt. This way I can eat a couple of cookies on the way back." He got up smoothly and left for the truck.

The phone beeped.

Go!

She took one last look in Hunter's direction, then picked up her backpack so that she had her phone and kept Austin's phone in her left hand and walked quickly toward the concession stand. Both new phones had tracking, she just needed to keep them with her.

As soon as she got past it, she saw the piece of shit Monte Carlo. She got in the passenger side door. There was a phone on the bench seat, and it was ringing; she answered it. As soon as she heard the raspy voice, she had to choke back bile and tears.

"Don't hurt Austin, you—"

"Don't anger me, Kenna. I might do something you won't like. I've got a rifle trained on him at this very moment."

She looked around. Where was he? How could he see her? Then she saw the little camera up above the rearview mirror.

"Kenna, what's in your hands?"

She looked down at her backpack and Austin's phone.

"Throw the phone and the backpack out the window now. They probably have trackers in them. We don't need your bodyguard finding you."

Kenna rolled down the window and threw them onto the cement of the parking lot, wincing when she heard Austin's cell phone shatter.

She swallowed a sob. "Good girl. Slide on over to the driver's seat and start the car. We're going for a drive."

* * *

Dex listened carefully to Hunter. His friend was clear and concise. As soon as the words, "Kenna is missing," were uttered, Dex was in an altered state. He was now a SEAL in the middle of a mission. Fear, panic, and guilt had no place for what needed to get done. Hunter was in the same mode.

"Somehow, he must have convinced her that he'd take out her mom or Austin," Dex said grimly.

"That's my take. But Wyatt called Penny, she's fine. She's also armed. Aiden's on his way there now."

"What do you know about Kenna's abduction?" Dex asked.

"We found her backpack and Austin's broken cell phone on the ground of the East parking lot, near the only empty parking space. I was parked in the West."

"Where is Austin?"

"We just got into my truck, and we're hauling ass to the base, he'll be safe there."

"As soon as you're done doing that. Meet back up at Jack's," Dex commanded. "I'm calling the two cops working the case. Gray is out with Captain Hale, but Griff and Dalton will be there too."

"Got it."

"Can I talk to Dex?" He heard Austin ask Hunter.

Hunter must have handed the phone over. "Dex." Austin's voice was shaky.

"I'm going to get her back."

He could hear the kid swallow. "You've got to do it fast," his words trembled.

"I'm going to."

There was a long pause. Dex needed to shut it down.

At last, Austin spoke again.

"I'm trusting you with my mother's life."

Ahh, fuck.

"I'm going to bring her home."

There was nothing but a dial tone.

* * *

He was past ninety miles an hour on the Five freeway. He'd be going faster if he could get past other drivers and he didn't think he'd get pulled over and cause a delay. Clint was talking on the speaker in his jeep.

"He texted Austin's phone."

Sanchez and Warren were conferenced in on the call. "How in the hell—" Clive started.

"Now we know how he got to her. Do you have transcripts of the text?" he asked Clint.

"Fuck Man, he was at Moonlight Beach, he sent a picture of Austin in a rifle's crosshairs." The killer said he'd kill the boy if she didn't leave with him. But I've got some good news. We're looking for a green Monte Carlo with a white vinyl top. That's the car he told her to go to in the parking lot."

"We'll get an APB immediately. We'll see what community and freeway cameras we can pull to grab a plate number. Is there anything else?" Sanchez asked.

"All five of those profiles started on the same date. I've been doing research on the founder of the company, to see if that got me anywhere. This was Lyle Gale's baby. He started it and sold it for a pretty profit thirteen months ago. Two days after new ownership took over, the five profiles showed up. New ownership was Kenna's friend, Buddy Finch."

"It's slim," Warren said.

"We can't get a search warrant on something like that. We need someone to take Buddy's picture and compare it to the tapes we pulled from the La Jolla Starbuck's, then we have enough for a warrant," Sanchez said.

Dex hit his steering wheel.

"Are you taking care of that?" Clint asked.

"We're on it," Warren said.

Dex ended the call. He couldn't stomach any more. They didn't have time for that kind of bullshit. His phone rang, he pressed the answer button on his steering wheel as he sped towards his exit.

"It's me," Clint said. "It's got to be Finch."

"Sounds like."

"I'll have his whole life's story waiting for you by the time you get to Jack's."

Dex prayed that Jack's house was a smart place to be and that he wasn't heading in the absolute wrong fucking direction! He slammed the wheel of his car again. Again.

"Dude? You with me?"

"Yeah," Dex said breathing through his nose.

"I'm going to hang up now. Drive safe. You getting in a wreck isn't going to help things."

"I don't need a mother or a fucking grandmother." He pressed end on the call but made sure he was on track enough to drive.

CHAPTER THIRTEEN

She slammed her hand against the steering wheel.

"Tsk Tsk, Kenna. Don't hurt yourself. That's for me to do."

She wasn't going to cry. It was useless. She needed to think. There wasn't a fucking chance in hell she was going to leave Austin without a mother. Her hands were slick with sweat. She was on Highway Fifty-Six, headed towards Poway. She'd been driving for what seemed like forever.

"Take the upcoming exit," the raspy voice said.

"Use your own voice. You don't have to hide any longer!" she shouted.

"I like this voice. Jean especially liked it. She said it was sexy."

Kenna heard herself whimper.

"Ooooh. I like that sound. Do it again."

Kenna blinked rapidly.

Don't cry, don't cry, don't cry. There's no crying in baseball. Don't let the whackjob see you cry.

"Whimper!"

"Go fuck yourself!"

"I'm going to fuck you."

God, she didn't even know if the women were raped or not. Had they been?

"Why are you doing this? Why me?"

"Because everybody wants you. Because you're the focus, and your death is going to matter."

"You're not making any sense."

"Go left at the bottom of the ramp."

"No. I'm going to pull over."

"I'm still here at the beach. I'll shoot Austin."

It was like a Rubik's cube. He had to have a GPS on the phone, plus he had a camera trained on her. Was he really at the beach? Wasn't he going to meet her at wherever she was headed? The fucker couldn't be at two places at once. Wait a minute, there wasn't a chance in hell Austin was still at the beach. Not if she had disappeared. Nope, Hunter would have been on the search for her in a heartbeat.

She saw a gas station to her right. Her fingers were clammy. Could she take the chance? She had to. She couldn't leave Austin without a mother. She couldn't. She veered over to the right, the car hopped up over the lip of the gas station entrance because she was going so fast. All of the pump stations were full.

Shit!

226 · CAITLYN O'LEARY

She pulled over to the side in front of the air station.

"What are you doing?" he yelled. "Get back on the road and turn around." The man's voice came in clearer. Did she recognize it?

"I want to see another photograph of Austin." What was the term? "I want proof that he's alive." That wasn't the term. "I want proof of life. That's it. I want proof of life!" she shouted into the phone.

"Show me my son!" she said stalling. "Send a picture of him to this phone."

The passenger door opened. She was facing a gun.

* * *

"He has a cabin at Big Bear, and his house in La Jolla," Clint said over the speaker on the Dex's cell phone. "Sanchez called, and they got a hit on the Monte Carlo heading east on the Fifty-Six, so both of those are out."

Ever since hearing that both of the phones with trackers had ended up on the Moonlight Beach parking lot and not with Kenna, Dex's mind had been going rapid fire, considering and discarding possible ways to find her or Buddy Finch. The man wasn't at his office at Genesee Executive Plaza, his secretary hadn't seen him since yesterday morning.

"Clint, does his company have any holdings? Any places he might have taken her?" Dex asked.

"For fuck's sake, of course, I looked. He has two small office buildings, both occupied. Nothing that could work.

Right now, I'm checking all of Rosalie's properties. That's more complicated."

"What the hell are you talking about?" Dex demanded.

"She had seven husbands. I have to go through seven different names. Do you know that she has thirteen step-kids? Buddy is her only living blood relative. Her son died, hence there's Buddy."

"I don't give a shit. Find me a place that is east of La Jolla that Buddy is using as a killing ground! Meanwhile, I'm going to check out his house and see if there are any clues there."

"Got it." Clint hung up.

Hunter was already at the door, and Dex was halfway to him when Penny called out to him from the other room. She had been staying in the living room, but it was obvious she had been listening in.

"Penny, I've got to go," he said distractedly.

"Wait. It's important." She rushed up beside him and grabbed his arm. She looked like she had aged twenty years. "I think somebody needs to talk to Rosalie and just ask her about the properties. She'd have the best idea where to look."

"Penny," Dex started.

"Rosalie's a big girl. If her grandson is involved, she'll want him caught. She'll want to help Kenna."

"We don't have time."

"You have to make time. I'm telling you, she'll tell you what you need to know."

"All right, I'll call her on the way to Buddy's house."

228 · CAITLYN O'LEARY

Penny squeezed his arm and shook her head. "A call won't get it done."

He hesitated.

"Goddammit, Dex. You know I'm right!" Shit, now he knew where Kenna got it from. She *was* right.

"Okay, I'll go now."

She gave a tight nod and let go of his arm. He went out the door. Hunter was in his truck and had it started up when he sprinted to his jeep. It didn't need to be said that they were going to take two vehicles in case they needed to split up. When he got in, he pulled out his phone. Dalton and Griff still hadn't arrived at Jack's house. They were minutes away.

"Griff, call Clint. He's going to give you directions to Buddy Finch's house in La Jolla. We're pretty damned sure he's the killer. We're also pretty damned sure his house is empty because he's got Kenna pointed towards Poway. But we need you to check it out. See if you can find anything that might lead us to where he's keeping her."

* * *

Dex thought Rosalie was going to pass out, but then she rallied.

"He's not a killer."

Hunter was looking at her, assessing.

"Rosalie, the evidence is looking like he is. We don't have enough to stand up in a court of law, or even get a search warrant at this point. That's not what we're asking for. We're not

cops. I'm asking as Kenna's man, for your help to find her before she winds up dead."

She was sitting on the pink sofa, looking frail but determined. Hunter was standing near the door, Dex was sitting
next to her. She grabbed his hand with a surprisingly firm
grip. "I'm not trying to plead his case. I just don't want you to
waste *a minute* on a wild goose chase, not with Kenna's life
hanging in the balance. Buddy has not killed anyone."

"Ma'am, everything started after Buddy bought the website. The e-mails all came from a Starbucks not far from his
house. The SDPD is working on finding footage of him
there. He hasn't been seen since yesterday morning. Do you
know where he is?" Dex kept his voice calm. Barely.

"Dex, there has to be another reason for this. It isn't him.
Something is wrong. He was supposed to be here last night.
He didn't call. I called his office this morning, and he didn't
show up or phone in. Wouldn't he do a better job of covering
his tracks if he was planning to murder Kenna? Wouldn't he
at least come up with a cover story?"

What she was saying made sense, but everything pointed
to Buddy. They didn't have anything else at the moment, they
needed to play this hand out. Still...

"Rosalie, I appreciate what you're saying. I do." He gave
her hand a light squeeze. "But right now, everything is
pointing toward him being our guy. Do you have any prop-
erty that he might use near Poway?"

She closed her eyes. A tear trickled down her cheek. Then she opened them. "I have three rental houses near Wildcat Canyon Road." She slowly pushed up from the couch.

"Stay there," Dex said. He immediately had his phone in his hand and dialed Clint.

"Yeah?" Clint answered.

"I've got Rosalie here, she said that she has three rental properties near Wildcat Canyon Road that might fill the bill."

"I haven't found those."

Dex put the phone on speaker. "Rosalie, tell Clint about the houses."

"They're three one-bedroom houses listed under the Sandrine Corporation. That was Rusty's corporation. It was such a pretty name, I haven't changed it."

"Buddy knows about the houses?" Clint asked.

"Yes. But he's not the man you're looking for. I know you have to look. I'm pretty sure two of the houses are not being rented right now. You can ask Buddy's secretary."

"Found it," Clint said. "I'm texting it to you and Hunter now."

Dex got up off the sofa, Hunter was opening the door to the office.

"Even though I think you're wrong, God speed."

Dex looked at Rosalie's face that for once looked its age. "Thank you."

* * *

"What?" Hunter asked as they ran to their vehicles.

Dex followed Hunter to his truck and watched as he got in. He spoke as Hunter buckled up. "I'm going to follow you to the houses, but I might pull off on the way."

"What the fuck?"

"She's right, somebody could be setting Buddy up, and this could be a red herring. I'm going to have Clint look at other angles, but I still want those goddamn rentals looked at no matter what. You're the man I trust to do it."

Hunter grunted.

Dex ran to his jeep and followed Hunter as he sped out of the circular drive.

* * *

It took everything she had to tear her gaze away from the gun as he slid in beside her.

"Look at me. I want you to acknowledge me," he said.

Her entire body trembled, the only thing keeping her together, were her hands on the steering wheel. She raised her head and looked at him. Who the hell was he? Whoever he was, he was angry. No, he was furious.

He shoved the gun into her ribs.

"Ow!"

"Shut up and put this piece of shit into reverse."

"Where did you come from?"

"I was following you. Do what I say, or I'll shoot you."

"No, you won't. You want to torture me." She'd had enough of this shit. Kenna turned to grab the door handle of the car.

"You're right, I do," he said dropping the gun and grabbing her hair. He held up a garage door opener and put it to her neck. Kenna felt the sharp electrical current going through her. Fuck, it was a stunner, not a garage door opener, she thought as he continued to hold it against her. She opened her mouth to scream, but nothing would come out.

She collapsed. Her eyes drifted shut. God, she was going to end up dying after all.

* * *

"We've got some proof," Griff's voice came over the speaker in Dex's jeep.

"What did you find?"

"There's pictures of Kenna plastered all over a small room in the basement. He's got a veritable shrine set up."

"You don't sound really happy," Dex said to Griff.

"It's Dalton. He'll explain."

"Hey, Dex," Dalton's smooth, thoughtful voice permeated the inside of his cab. "I think we need C.S.I. to come out and look at this. There are some anomalies."

"Dammit, Dal, I don't have time for you to be absolutely fucking sure. What are you seeing? What are you sensing? I would take your intuition over a C.S.I. report any goddamn day!"

"Okay," Dalton said and blew out a breath. "To start with some of the pictures are old. They've obviously been taken over the last year and printed out. You can see where they've faded with time. But all of the tape that was used to adhere the pictures to the wall? It's new. None of it is faded. If I had to guess, these photos were taped up in the last few days, if not the last day. I think these were brought here from some-place else."

"You think it's a set-up?"

"That's what my gut is telling me."

"Tear that fucking house apart. If it *is* a set-up, then Buddy's a victim too. In the meantime, I'm calling Clint. There has to be somebody else who would tie in both Buddy and Kenna."

"Gotchya. We'll call if we find anything."

Dex hit the steering wheel...again. Then pressed in Clint's number. He relayed what Griff and Dalton had found.

"Are you coming back towards La Jolla or San Diego?" Clint asked.

"No, she was last seen heading east, this is as good as direc-tion as any. I need you to tear Buddy's e-mail accounts apart."

"It's already hacked," Clint said. "I was trying to see if he was sending any e-mails to any of the victims, or if he had set up any new accounts. I've cloned his entire office network."

Dex gave a low whistle. "Did you check his incoming e-mails?"

There was a pause. "Nope. Been looking at his outgoing."

"Check his incoming. See if Buddy has any enemies. See if the Starbucks IP address ever sent an e-mail *to* Buddy."

"I'm on it."

After the call disconnected, he stared at Hunter's electric blue truck in front of him. There had to be a connection somewhere, and he just wasn't seeing it.

* * *

She ached all over. She smelled the distinct odor of blood, decaying flesh, and bleach. She kept her eyes closed, wanting to take in as much information as her other senses could, without alerting the killer that she was awake.

"I know you're awake."

She didn't move. Her hands were tied behind her. Her shoulders felt like they were being ripped out their sockets.

"You snore."

She so didn't snore!

She felt the toe of a shoe or boot pushing at her hip, rocking her back and forth.

"Open your eyes, or I'll kick you."

She kept her eyes closed.

The shoe stopped prodding her. She heard steps, then a meaty thud.

"Ahhhhhh!" a man screamed. Her eyes shot open.

"I knew you were awake."

Kenna looked up into the nondescript face of a monster. He was laughing. He kicked Buddy again, and this time her friend just groaned in pain.

"Get up, Kenna. I have a special seat for you."

"I'm not going to do one goddamn thing you ask. My son is safe," she ground out.

"But you like him, don't you? He likes you. He bought a company for you. You don't want to see good ole Buddy Finch hurt, now do you? Get in the fucking chair!"

"Don't do it," Buddy gasped. The man reared back and kicked Buddy in his head, and he slumped into silence.

"Now get in the chair." The monster pointed to a ladder-back chair in the middle of the room. It was dim. There were mounds of what looked like trash pushed up against two of the walls, all of it covered in clear plastic. She looked closer and saw the outline of a human hand pressed up against one of the plastic tarps.

This was it. Her future.

"I said. Get in the chair."

"You're not very bright, are you? Once again, you've lost your leverage."

Go big or go home.

"What did you say to me?" There was the raspy and creepy tone of voice again.

"That was a killing blow," Kenna said disgustedly. "Now you're going to kill me. I'm not going to do a goddamn thing that you tell me to do."

She saw his eyes dart to where Buddy was lying on the floor. He looked unsure. She'd scored a point.

"He's not dead, you bitch," the man snarled at her.

"If he's not dead now, he will be shortly. Look at him, he's going to aspirate on his own vomit." She said it like she didn't care.

"What?"

"He's going to choke. He's going to choke on his own vomit and die." Kenna's tone was filled with derision.

Killer boy took three long steps toward her and swung. She didn't even see his fist coming. She'd been propped up on her shoulder, but now she was laid out flat, her ears ringing, blood dripping from her nose.

"You're a nurse. Fix him!"

"You beat me up, how can I fix him?" *Don't say dumbass, don't say dumbass.* "Dumbass," she muttered.

"I will kill you if you don't do what I say!" he roared.

"For fuck's sake, you're already planning on killing me!" she screamed at him.

Stop it. Think of Austin. Don't give up.

He pulled out a knife. "Kenna, you're the one I've always wanted. If you're nice, you don't have to die." He knelt down and sun coming through the one window in the big room glinted off the steel blade. That was the moment when Kenna realized she wasn't as brave as her mouth was. She cringed backwards. He leaned over her and cut the zip tie holding her hands together.

She yelped with pain as the circulation started back in her hands, arms, and shoulders. He shoved her towards Buddy.

"Go help him. I want him to live. He needs to see what I'm going to do to you."

Kenna hurt, and it didn't feel like her body was under her control, but somehow, she was able to get on her knees and scuffle over to Buddy. She practically fell on top of him. His breathing was labored, but he wasn't choking.

She put two fingers to his neck to feel his pulse. Thank God. It was strong.

Kenna put her mouth to his ear. "Buddy, can you open your eyes? Please. I need to see your eyes."

"Stop whispering, Bitch!"

"Who are you?" She threw the question over her shoulder.

"Lyle. It's Lyle," Buddy whispered as he opened his eyes.

She looked at his blue eyes. She thanked God again. Both of his pupils were equal.

"He's not dead. He's not choking. Let the games begin. Kenna, get into the chair."

Kenna had been looking around the room and realized they were in a home's empty garage. Lyle, if that was his name, was standing in front of the bay door, behind her was the door leading to the house. She scrambled to her feet and ran towards the door.

"Got you," he said with glee as he wrenched a handful of her hair and pulled her away from the door. She jerked back, not caring about the pain. Barely, just barely, she managed to press the button that opened the garage door. The motor started to rumble.

"You bitch."

He threw her to the floor, but she grabbed his leg, doing anything she could think of to stop him from pressing the switch. He kicked out at her, but she held on like a tick on a hound.

"Let go!"

She saw sunlight coming in underneath the bay door. He kicked out again, and she lost her hold. The rumble stopped. She saw that the door had only gone up maybe three feet.

"Help!" she screamed at the top of her lungs. Praying God some neighbor would hear.

She watched as he pressed the button again, and the door began its descent.

"Help!"

"Nobody can hear you, dear," he said as he cupped her cheek.

She jerked her head out of his grip, but he was ready for her. He yanked on her hair and dragged her to the middle of the room.

Please God, give me strength until Dex finds me.

CHAPTER FOURTEEN

Traffic was bad. They were down to eighteen miles an hour. It was giving Dex plenty of time to think.

Why would Buddy and Kenna both be targets over that fucking dating site, if Buddy didn't have a profile, or did he? It all begins and ends with that stupid fucking site!

He called Clint.

Before Dex even asked a question, Clint started talking. "I haven't found any e-mails coming into Buddy's accounts from the Starbuck's IP address. Now I'm going through his less than stellar fan mail. It's the usual bullshit crap in business. He's made a couple of special fans."

"You're kidding, right? Buddy seems so likeable."

"There's this one guy that swears he stole his company out from under him. He's fucking pissed. Or he was," Clint said.

"Gates! I know him. Buddy mentioned him at a barbecue."

"Gale. Lyle Gale. Yeah, there have been a few back thirteen months ago. They've tapered down."

"That's our guy!"

"What the fuck are you talking about? Are you sure, Dex?"

"It all makes sense. The killing centers around the site but started when Buddy ripped the company out of this guy's hands. Let me guess, the e-mails from Lyle were over the top."

"Yeah, they were," Clint conceded.

"This guy had to have figured out that Buddy was doing this to check-up on Kenna, so Kenna became a focus. He's been e-mailing her since the takeover."

"Why kill the other women?"

"I don't know about the first, but Jean was clearly a message to Kenna, so was this last one where he sent video. My bet is that we'll find a connection between the first and Kenna if we look. But we don't have time right now. Find Lyle's properties."

"Stay on the line, I'm doing it right now."

"At last. We're finally getting off this fucking freeway."

He followed Hunter down the exit ramp, past the gas station, and took a left through the light. They got lucky, and there was a break in traffic. He could hear the tapping of Clint's computer keys as they drove fast through the sparsely populated area leading to Wildcat Canyon.

It was killing him driving there, but where else did they have to go at the moment? It was still possible he was wrong, and Buddy was the killer. If Lyle's properties were in La Jolla, then Dalton and Griff were there if it was San Diego, then Clint and Aiden were there.

"You have got to be shitting me."

"What?" Dex asked Clint.

"The one house of Rosalie's that's being rented in Wildcat Canyon?"

"Yeah?"

"It's got Lyle Gale's name on the lease," Clint said.

Hunter was already going twice the legal limit on the road. Dex stomped on the accelerator and roared past him.

* * *

She'd thought he'd strip her. But she was still wearing her blouse and jeans. He'd used rope, not zip ties, to tie her to the chair. When she tried to tip it over, she realized it was bolted to the cement floor.

"Ah Kenna, this is a pro operation. If the chair fell over, I couldn't have my fun."

She watched as he went over to a table near one of the plastic tarps. Now that she wasn't fighting him, the smell was even worse. Or maybe she was just imagining her body being under one of the tarps, and that's what made her gag. Lyle picked up something up. He turned back to her, and she watched as he put on a mask.

"Thank you." She smiled.

His step faltered as he walked back to her. She ignored the whip in his hand.

"What are you thanking me for?"

"I couldn't stand seeing your ugly face anymore, so thanks for covering it up."

She might not be able to fight with her body, but nothing was going to stop her from fighting with her words.

"Stop it, Kenna." Buddy's voice was a tortured whisper.

Lyle slowly uncoiled the whip. He held it over his head before she braced she had to get in one last dig.

"Why should I stop speaking the truth? He's an ugly man."

He threw the whip down on the ground.

"You bitch. I have just the thing to shut you up."

He whirled back to the table and came back holding a dog collar, but it looked weird, it had something connected to it. He unhooked it and slapped it around her neck, tightening it to the point she thought she might choke. "There. That should do it."

"You can't even do that right. I can still talk, you pussy."

Through the leather mask, she saw his gray eyes, and his thick lips smile. He held up walkie talky device. "Did you just call me a pussy?"

"I call them like I see them." Her voice was hoarse because of the collar, but she forced her own smile.

His thumb hit the button on the device.

A charge of electricity shot through the collar. In horror, she watched as he continued to hold down the button and red anguish took over her mind.

Was that wail of pain coming from her?

"So beautiful."

She couldn't see.

Open your eyes.

She tried to swallow, but her mouth felt like it was full of cotton. She spoke anyway. "Sure, since you can't get it up. I suppose you have to shock me. Have at it."

Everything went red, then white.

She needed him to untie her. If he tried to rape her, he'd untie her. It was the only thought going through her brain besides the pain.

She heard a grunt and a thump. She forced her head up. It hurt to move, but she looked and saw Buddy grappling with Lyle on the floor.

Her head dropped. The pain was excruciating. Even if he did untie her, could she do anything to help herself?

Ewww. Drool.

* * *

The houses didn't have house numbers on them. All three were clustered together at the end of a desolate cul-de-sac and looked damn near identical. It didn't matter, there was a green Monte Carlo parked in front of the middle one.

Dex parked down the street, Hunter pulled in behind him. He took his Sig Sauer handgun from his glove box.

"Front or back?" Hunter asked. He was holding a gun as well.

"I'll take the back," Dex said.

Hunter nodded.

They took off.

It was a small house, only one-bedroom window to look in, and it was empty, so was the kitchen, dining room and living room. He could see Hunter peering in through the plate glass window at the front of the house. When Dex tried to open the sliding glass door, it was locked. The only place left was the garage. He could see the door to the garage from where he stood. He didn't want to break any glass because he was afraid they'd be heard.

He looked up to see Hunter striding across the living room towards him. He'd gotten the front door open. Probably picked the lock. He'd forgotten Hunter's wayward past. When they were both inside the house, they went to the door leading to the garage and listened. They heard a muffled noise.

Dex nodded as his hand turned the knob.

In an instant, he took in the scene. It was the same room where the woman had been whipped to death. Kenna was slumped forward in the same chair. A man in a mask was kicking another man on the floor. He looked up at Hunter and Dex.

"Stop right there." He held up the remote control device for a shock collar. He could see it connected around Kenna's neck. "I've got it ramped up to the highest level. I'll kill her."

Dex looked at him and looked at Kenna. Her eyes were looking up at him. She was pissed. He loved her. He turned back to Lyle and shot him between the eyes.

His eyes quickly swept the big room, there was no one else. Just the victim on the floor, the killer, and Kenna. He was at the chair in an instant. She was trying to look up.

"Hold on, Baby," he crooned gently as he cupped her jaw and tilted her head so he could see how the collar was attached. It was so goddamned tight. His fingers went to work to get it undone, and she whimpered.

"I know it hurts, I'm so sorry."

"Doesn't matter," she croaked. "Buddy?" He looked over his head and saw Hunter attending to him.

"He's going to be fine." Dex hoped he wasn't lying.

"Is Austin okay?"

She squeaked with pain as he pressed in to unclasp the collar. "It's off."

"How's Austin?" she asked, undeterred. She couldn't even lift her head on her own, and she was in mama bear mode.

"He's fine, Kenna. He's at the base."

She slumped forward in the ropes. Dex was horrified by what he saw on her neck.

"Did you call an ambulance?" he shouted to Hunter.

"They're on their way, so are the cops."

"Let me see to Buddy. Get these ropes off me." She struggled.

"Kenna, stop! You're making it worse." He had his knife out and was cutting the ropes off her feet. "If you keep trying to kick, I might cut you."

"You'd never cut me. Now hurry up." Her voice sounded like a frog's, but she was giving him shit.

He got the last rope off her body, and she slid into his arms, she was too weak to do anything else but rest.

"I'm a nurse, I need to get to Buddy. He saved me." Her voice was filled with tears.

"You saved me," Buddy whispered from across the room.

She shuddered in his arms.

See he's talking. He's going to be all right," Dex assured her.

Dex heard the sirens.

* * *

She hung up the hospital room phone. She'd finally gotten Rosalie to laugh. It had taken a lot. Now she was exhausted. Dex was glowering at her.

"What?"

"Stop trying to make everybody else feel better."

"Now that she knows Buddy is doing well, Rosalie is intent on doing as much as she can for Lyle's victims. She's sure it is all her fault for forcing Buddy to buy Lyle's company, and she's paying for the funeral services and—"

Dex drove his fists on either side of her waist, and his face stopped inches from hers. "The only victim I give a shit about is you."

"She's a victim too. Buddy almost died. Her grandson almost died. She feels terrible."

"He was a whackjob, Kenna. You can't predict crazy." Dex kissed her forehead. "You're going to be here two more days, and instead of recovering I've seen you do nothing but try to make your mom, your son, Rosalie, and your co-workers feel better. You can worry about Austin, but nobody else. Especially me."

"What are you talking about?" She scowled. "I've been a basket case around you."

He slid his big hand under her back and hugged her close. "Do you know how scared I was at the thought of losing you? And now all you've tried to reassure me that you're all right, instead of giving yourself the greenlight to have a meltdown."

"Well, I am all right!" She pushed against him. "I survived."

He pressed the softest kiss she'd ever felt against her neck. Tears pricked her eyes. "Of course, you survived, Kenna. You're a survivor. Now lean on me. Can you do that?"

A tear trickled down her face. Could she? What happened if she leaned and then he went away, she would never stop falling. *That* she couldn't survive.

Stop that. Those are old tapes, Kenna Leigh! This man is your own personal hero!

He moved his head so he could look into her eyes. "My life almost ended two days ago. You're my everything. I want to be here for you."

She looked into those diamond bright brown eyes and saw a new truth and the start of a new life for herself. She had somebody who loved her, somebody she could trust to take care of her heart.

"I'll lean on you until the day I die," she promised.

"Thank God."

EPILOGUE

It had taken two months for Kenna to convince everybody that she was all right. Austin was the last hold-out. It turned out that he had watched too damned much of that fucking video to be placated with anything but the truth. Kenna sat on the picnic table at Moonlight Beach and watched her son up on his feet on the surfboard and thought about that conversation they'd had last week.

It'd been after a wrestling match where Austin had been called for unnecessary roughness, something that had never happened before. She could tell he was horrified because afterwards, he immediately let himself get pinned. On the ride home, she couldn't get him to open up. When they got home, he went straight to his room.

It was one of the few times that Dex wasn't spending the night, and Kenna was wound tight. She had trouble sleeping when he wasn't there, so that night she was up watching a movie when Austin came downstairs.

"Mom, we need to talk." He didn't sit down beside her on the couch. Instead, he chose the recliner, and he sat forward, hands clasped in front of him. Kenna sat up.

"What is it?"

"I've heard you crying."

Oh fuck.

He continued. "You've never come clean about that day."

"Austin, I told you most of it," she said slowly.

He looked up at her, his gaze solemn. "Dex is helping you with it. I know he is. You're starting to heal. But I want to be there for you too."

A sob bubbled up before she could contain it. Austin was out of his chair and beside her on the couch in an instant.

"Tell me."

She was never going to tell her child everything that happened. But Christ on a cracker, could she have a better child?

"I'm not going to tell you everything. I'm just not, Austin."

"You have to."

She smiled through the wet and put her forehead against his. "Honey, it's like Dex said, there are going to be enough scars on your soul eventually. What I will tell you, is that it was the thought of you that got me through that hell. I didn't give up because of you."

He put his big hands on her shoulders. "I thank God Dex was there to save you that day. I'm glad you're going to have him when I leave one day, but you can't shut me out."

Her eyes got wide. "That's not what I'm doing."

"Aren't you?"

Shit. Did she raise the Dali Lama?

"You're something else," she whispered.

"Since you can't sleep, and you won't talk, want me to make some popcorn?"

"Bullshit, I want chocolate pudding, with condensed milk poured on top," Kenna said.

"Score!" Austin said as he bounded off the couch.

* * *

Dex watched Kenna sleep. She was restless, and he hated that. He pulled her closer and feathered a kiss against her temple.

"Shhh, Baby, I've got you. You're safe." Somewhere deep in her subconscious, she must have heard him because she settled. He brushed his fingers over her neck. If he lived to be a hundred, he would never forget that frantic minute it took to get that fucking collar off her. Then seeing the bruises and blisters had made him want to kill Gale all over again, only more slowly, more painfully.

Kenna absolutely amazed him. That day, she could barely move, and her only thought was to help Buddy. Hunter was still talking about it, and Hunter hardly talked.

Seven days out of the hospital and Kenna was taking things on full tilt. She informed him she was seeing a psychologist twice a week to 'get that fucking whackjob out of my head.' It helped that Penny was a strong shoulder for her daughter to lean on, but Dex knew even without her, Kenna would have been able to cope. That was who she was.

She said something in her sleep.

"What, Baby?"

"Dex?"

"I'm here."

"Good. Go to sleep, Honey." She tugged him closer, and he smiled. He watched as her eyes drifted shut and she fell back asleep.

She even worried about him. There was the serious conversation she tried to have where she wanted to talk about how shooting Lyle might have adversely affected him. It was the first time he'd really laughed since she'd gone missing that day.

"Poppy," he remembered saying. "Killing Lyle Gale wasn't even a blip on my radar. All that mattered was getting to you, and he was in the way."

"But he—"

Dex interrupted. "After I really got a chance to see the house of horrors, and realize that there were two bodies in there, my level of satisfaction quadrupled. Are you going to tell me you wouldn't have wanted to pull that trigger?"

Her face had hardened.

"I would have aimed for his dick and let him bleed out."

He loved his vicious woman, and he told her so.

She cried. "I hate crying," she said into his shirt.

"I love that you're *here* to cry. Let it out, Baby."

She did that day. But those were the early weeks. Now, she smiled and only sometimes had a nightmare. His woman was phenomenal.

* * *

She watched as Dex walked down the beach from the parking lot. He was bringing the blanket from his jeep, along with a thermos of hot chocolate. She saw a pink box of donuts too. Hopefully, there were some chocolate ones with sprinkles. She liked being pampered with chocolate. Hell, she just liked being pampered. Who knew that could ever happen for her?

"He's doing good. I saw him catch a wave," he commented as he settled the blanket around her shoulders.

"That's my boy."

"You've raised a wonderful son." Dex kissed her temple. Tears threatened, but she held them back. Hell, was there a better compliment?

"Yeah well, you should try going on a drive with him, then you wouldn't think he was all that fired wonderful," she muttered.

"He's a great driver."

She slid Dex a side-long glance. "Oh yeah, you went driving with him on the range," she remembered.

"Huh?"

"He told me how you two were going to the driving range."

"Yeah. He came out to the driving range with Gramps and me while you were at Rosalie's. I thought he told you." He paused and looked at her, then started laughing. "You do know that the driving range is where you go to hit practice golf balls, don't you?"

"Oh shit. For real?"

"Yep." He was still chuckling, the bastard. She loved it when he laughed. Dex Evans was a handsome man, but when he laughed, he was devastating. He must have seen her staring because he cupped the side of her face and dipped in for a kiss.

Kenna's tummy melted as his tongue traced her lower lip, then pressed inside. A kiss on the beach at dawn. He continued to give her the best memories imaginable. He lifted his head and rubbed his nose against hers.

"I love you, Kenna. The luckiest day of my life was when I read your snarky e-mail."

Her cheeks heated. He mentioned that e-mail a lot. She'd gone back and read it. She'd actually talked about her panties getting damp. If it weren't for the fact it snagged her a reply, she'd find herself a hole and start covering herself with dirt.

"You're blushing. Are your panties damp?" he teased.

"Kiss me again." She arched up and met his lips. After long moments, long, lush moments, yes, her panties were damp. Not that she would admit it. His eyes sparkled as he looked down at her.

"Are you ready for tonight?" he asked.

"A barbeque with the entire Evans clan. Including your parents? I'm not sure. But they better be nice. If they aren't, I'm going to kick some ass."

"I'm over that, Baby. But it's a nice thought."

She paused and looked at him. "Are you sure you're ready?"

"I'm positive. I have you by my side. You're such a mama bear. If I were ever lucky enough to have a child, I would want you to be their mother."

He hadn't said that, had he?

"Dex?"

He took her hand in his and laced their fingers together. Then he brought their hands to press them to his heart. "A while ago, I asked you to trust me with a little piece of your heart. Now I'm asking you to trust me with so much more."

"I would love to have children with you, but you've got it wrong. You're the one who's going to be the amazing parent."

She watched as he opened the pink box.

"Are we sealing the deal with donuts? If so, I want chocolate."

He pulled out a small black box. It was covered in powdered sugar. Even better. Her hand trembled in his. He held on tighter.

"I promise you'll be safe with me, Kenna. I'll never betray your trust. I'll cherish your feelings and listen to what you have to say. I love your son. I will attempt to bring beauty into every day of your life going forward. Will you marry me?"

He flipped open the latch on the box, and she saw the perfect ring. The marquis diamond was set in yellow gold to match the gold four leaf clover charm her dad had given her.

He waited. Dex knew her. He understood that she was having trouble catching her breath.

"Yes," she said. "Nobody deserves to be loved as much as you do, except our children. The only reason they'll get more love Dex is because it will be two of us giving it to them."

She untangled her hands from his and held out her left hand. "Put it on." He slid the beautiful ring on her finger, and it was like a place that had been shut down for too long finally was seeing the light. She threw her arms around his neck.

"I love you, Kenna."

"I love you back. Expect to have love rained down on your ass every day of your life, SailorBoy."

He threw back his head and laughed. "You're such a romantic."

The End

BIOGRAPHY

Caitlyn O'Leary is an avid reader and considers herself a fan first and an author second. She reads a wide variety of genres but finds herself going back to happily-ever-afters. Getting a chance to write, after years in corporate America, is a dream come true. She hopes her stories provide the kind of entertainment and escape she has found from some of her favorite authors.

Keep up with Caitlyn O'Leary:

Facebook: http://tinyurl.com/nuhvey2
Twitter: http://twitter.com/CaitlynOLearyNA
Pinterest: http://tinyurl.com/q36uohc
Goodreads: http://tinyurl.com/nqy66h7
Website: http://www.caitlynoleary.com
Email: caitlyn@caitlynoleary.com
Newsletter: http://bit.ly/1WIhRup
Instagram: http://bit.ly/29WaNIh

BOOKS BY CAITLYN O'LEARY

The Found Series
Revealed, Book One
Forsaken, Book Two
Healed, Book Three
Beloved, Book Four (Coming Soon)

Midnight Delta Series
Her Vigilant SEAL, Book One
Her Loyal SEAL, Book Two
Her Adoring SEAL, Book Three
Sealed with a Kiss, A Midnight Delta Novella, Book Four
Her Daring SEAL, Book Five
Her Fierce SEAL, Book Six
Protecting Hope, Book Seven
(*Seal of Protection & Midnight Delta Crossover Novel
Susan Stoker Kindle World*)
A SEAL's Vigilant Heart, Book Eight
Her Dominant SEAL, Book Nine
Her Relentless SEAL, Book Ten

Black Dawn Series
Her Steadfast HERO, Book One
Her Devoted HERO, Book Two

Shadow Alliance
Declan, Book One
Cooper's Promise, Book Two
(*Omega Team and Shadow Alliance Crossover Novel
Desiree Holt Kindle World*)

Fate Harbor Series Published by Siren/Bookstrand
Trusting Chance, Book One
Protecting Olivia, Book Two
Claiming Kara, Book Three
Isabella's Submission, Book Four
Cherishing Brianna, Book Five